By Michael Twist

ISBN: 978-0988534445

This book is a work of fiction. Any resemblance to actual events, or persons, either living or dead, is purely coincidental.

Table of Contents

Foreword

Touch of Beyond dabbles in that which is quite possibly beyond both our understanding and abilities. It was my intent to do so in a fashion that was closer to *under* than *over*-the-top, leaving much for the imagination in the way that movies of old required our filling in a blank or two.
M.T.

Picture Windows

People suspect I'm not much of a thinker. And I'll admit, my mind's not what it once was any more than my body is, but I'm convinced my mind's still sound, even if I do keep most thoughts to myself these days. I do some of my best thinking at night, on walks with Rex, where it's dark, cool, and quiet, the neighborhood settling down for the evening after a bustling day. We take our stroll after dinner, *Jeopardy*, and one of the various hour-long crime shows featuring brilliant detective work by socially awkward but inordinately attractive agents. Rex knows the routine well; leash, coat, hat, gloves, and a plastic bag for droppings. On rare occasions an umbrella is needed, making for some awkward handling with a loaded plastic bag, leash, and umbrella handle balanced between two often gloved and always arthritic hands.

Margaret, Rex, and I were the first to live in our brand new single-level duplex that borders an older neighborhood. Margaret had insisted on down-sizing after the kids had finally all moved out, saying she wanted less space to clean and a dog that wouldn't talk back or eat us out of house and home. I think the real reason had to do with a fall she had taken on a short flight of stairs, but the reason doesn't really matter because the duplex is perfectly accommodating.

It is chilly outside, and we are greeted with a faint breeze distributing an abundance of vibrant smells not unlike most neighborhoods with grass and shrubs where cats, dogs, kids, and vehicles congregate. The sky is clear, with stars shining through the mostly empty branches of the mature oak trees that line the street. Most weekends see people raking leaves, with another accumulation ready for oversized black garbage bags or burn piles by the time the next Saturday rolls around. I love fall and all the smells that accompany it, including the smoldering of leaves and yard debris for several days, even after a fire's been doused.

We walk slowly through the neighborhood, Rex seemingly at peace with the pace, rarely pulling on the leash, since he's nearly as long in the tooth as I am. Neither of us moves quite like we used to. I enjoy the pace, though, as it gives me a chance to study the neighbors who have left their curtains or blinds open. Big picture windows reveal living rooms like aquariums, with both the living and deceased swirling around and through one another, peacefully coexisting in houses that often serve as their only common link. The living are seemingly unaware of the dead, and the dead appear entirely untroubled by the living, as they often occupy the same furniture simultaneously. I suppose I should be grateful I can't see into any bedrooms.

Some of the homes are considerably more crowded than others, a phenomenon I'm not entirely convinced I understand, although I've formed a theory. I've come to suspect that the spirits or specters going about their business - possibly even the routines they held when still among the living - are those who died in the home or for whom the dwelling was their last real address. Mrs. Weathers, for example, can be seen knitting in front of the television in the home she lived in on Sycamore Street for thirty-three years before going to the nursing home where she died less than a month later. Alice and John Remington came to our home for dinner shortly thereafter, and Alice mentioned how poor, dementia-plagued Janice Page, who had gone to live with her daughter in Des Moines some five years ago, had finally passed. Every night for months after hearing this I looked for Janice through curtains, once hers, that were open more often than not. I failed to find her but would bet I could see her through her daughter's Des Moines windows if given the chance. I could well be wrong, but I don't know how else to explain why some houses are so much more active and occupied than others.

Strange is the way some of the houses have drawn similar families and personalities over the years. 1402 Chestnut, where the Fitzgeralds currently reside, features two disheveled middle-aged men who rage drunkenly about the house wearing grungy, sleeveless white undershirts. At first I thought they must be brothers who had lived together, but I saw them chasing women who could only be their wives, and the women's clothing definitely suggested different eras. I mention this only because Fitzgerald himself sits most nights in front of the television with a can of Schlitz never in danger of growing cold on a small table at his side, while the pale blue light from the set dances on the popcorn ceiling above him.

One home on Sequoia Street houses three widows, two of the women are inevitably reading while the third cross-stitches. Mr. and Mrs. Collier currently call the place home, but the missus, who was a voracious reader until her eyes began to fail, is on oxygen and sports a pallor that doesn't look long for this world. The same Alice Remington commented that Mr. Collier has already planned to move in with his brother's family after the inevitable takes place.

Of course, not all houses share inexplicable similarities. Most of the rooms I can see into are busy with mostly elderly people coming and going, shuffling about, laughing, playing cribbage, eating, drinking, or just talking on phones with curly cords. Their attire differs, but the mannerisms and habits are largely the same, people being people, regardless of time.

As we near our traditional turnaround point, Rex darts toward the narrow path between houses at the end of the cul-de-sac. I follow reluctantly. This is the shortcut kids use when heading toward the middle school soccer field that backs up to the development. When Rex is out of sight he looks around nervously before proceeding to urinate against a sapling. He's actually more modest than I am, and I chuckle to myself as we head back up the trail to the bulbous shape of the cul-de-sac. I notice the old boy needs to urinate much more often these days, and I wonder if there's some kind of prostate issue in play.

We take the Elm Street route home, which always saddens me because of the lime-colored house we pass where two boys roughly eight and ten years of age play checkers every night in front of the fireplace, ignored by the current family that spends most of its time in rooms other than their living room. Each boy wears a pair of overalls with one strap undone over dingy-white long-sleeved thermal underwear. It's clear they are brothers, but it's unclear what caused their early demise, and I try not to speculate.

Rex and I pick up the pace a bit as we are able to see our duplex after rounding the corner of Hemlock and Pine. I often wonder if Rex can see what I see in the windows of these homes. I try to remember when I first began to see the dead mingling among the living. I know I never saw this around the countryside where I was born and lived while I was young. But then again, my family built the home we lived in, and so far as I know, no one ever died there during my youth.

The walk ends on a good note, as I am always able to see into Mrs. Kindell's kitchen. Everything about her demeanor suggests she is happy, from the expression on her face to the brisk movements she makes while sifting flour or taking a prize-winning pie out of the oven. I strain to hear the song she's singing and can't, but the thought buoys my spirits all the same. The gravy on a good walk comes in the form of a cat I've dubbed *Sour Puss*, which always hisses at us before darting through a hole in the fence and retreating into the night.

When we enter our home I can see Margaret bustling from the bathroom to the bedroom in her bathrobe, rubbing lotion into her desiccated hands while she glides from room to room. She always seems to be doing two things at once, whereas I'm lucky to have the energy to do even one. I think about the love I have for her and hope I never return from a walk to see her ethereal form through the front room window of our duplex. Rex looks at me, and for a fleeting moment I suspect he is thinking the same thing.

A creature of habit, Rex knows the routine well: lock front door, hang up leash, set alarm, and kick off shoes. I smell the smoke from the backyard leaf burning in my coat as Rex takes off his. I then saunter into the bedroom and assume my rightful place on the bed at Margaret's feet.

Just Wait

At nine years of age, Kathy Moller had looked into the mirror and wondered what she would look like when grown up. Having just turned fourteen, she still looked into the mirror but no longer wondered. What you see is what you get, her Grandma May had told Kathy not long after her flow had started. What Kathy saw in the mirror was rather plain in her estimation - definitely not cute like Lisa Harris or Bea MacIntire. She eyed her modest bosom and thought, definitely not like Hailey Martin, either. With dark hair, pale skin, and an upper lip in need of a light monthly grazing, Kathy knew she was the kind of girl that would make a stable wife, but was hardly the head-turner that captivated the attention of teenage boys of the day. This verdict she had begun subscribing to after overhearing her mother say as much to Grandma May: *she may not look like much now, but that girl will turn out special; just wait.* But still, Kathy thought as she gazed into the mirror before meeting her friends on Halloween night; I am special, nonetheless. With this, she smiled into the mirror, blew herself a kiss, and turned off the light.

The four girls, all students in Mrs. Regal's first period English class, had decided not to wear costumes for the first Halloween since they had begun going to the carnival rather than trick-or-treating as they had as elementary schoolers. Instead, they had agreed to wear jeans and hooded sweatshirts. The sweatshirt Kathy had planned on wearing was sitting in a wet ball in the dryer, which had not been turned on. She wailed at Grandma

May for the oversight, insisting that it was important to fit in with her new friends, but it was too late for the garment to be dried, and her grandmother wouldn't let her wear the thing wet, or even damp. Pressed for time, Kathy opted for a pink sweater, which was very comfortable but a bit childish in her estimation. She hoped Hailey, Bea, and Lisa wouldn't notice.

"Nice sweater. I thought all we agreed on sweatshirts," Lisa chimed, upon seeing Kathy at the corner on which they had agreed to meet.

Kathy briefly wondered how many pieces of gum comprised the green wad visible in Lisa's mouth when she spoke and sometimes even when she did not. "My mom forgot to dry the sweatshirt I was going to wear," Kathy began to explain.

"Why din'tcha just wear another?" Bea asked, her wad blue.

Kathy had known it would be hard to keep up with this group from the beginning. They all had numerous sweatshirts, not to mention fathers supporting their families, while she had a mother who took on every shift she could waiting tables and a grandmother that more or less took care of the home front. Bea, Hailey, and Lisa had taken Kathy into their small group after the late summer move-in had demonstrated a tendency to take on the lion's share of group work on both social studies and science projects during the first quarter, leaving them with little more than deciphering Kathy's horrendous handwriting while writing the final paper. "I was in a hurry and grabbed any old thing, and this is what I came up with," Kathy explained, trying to sound casual. "Probably the last time I'll ever wear it," she added.

"Yeah," Hailey said, fortifying her wad (pink) with yet another stick of gum using fingers that ended with festive black polish. "Boobs are a real game changer."

"You'd know," Lisa giggled.

"Right you are," Hailey smirked.

"That probably explains why you're always on the phone with Kevin Steele," Bea teased.

"*That*? You mean *they*," Lisa corrected.

"*They* explain a lot of things. And *that's* all I'm going to say on *that* subject," Hailey beamed, as the girls began walking in the direction of the carnival.

A brittle wind picked up and began to usher the girls along with scads of fallen leaves in the direction of the bright lights and music that could be heard from several blocks away. Dozens of trick-or-treaters, most of them younger and dressed as princesses, witches, mummies, pirates, and vampires, made their way through the established neighborhood in small groups, each carrying bags that grew heavier as the night progressed. Overhead, the mature elms and maples cast dark shifting silhouettes against a brooding sky.

After shelling out two dollars apiece for multi-colored swirls of cotton candy, the quartet headed for Prize Alley which consisted of games of skill and chance, most of which sported terrible odds for any participant willing to part with a dollar or two in hopes of winning a stuffed animal, colorful glass stein, or oversized helium filled balloon. Softball tosses, modified BB gun ranges, hammer meters, and shallow dish receptacles all beckoned at the behest of scraggly but persistent vendors. Intermittent shrieking broke through the piped-in midway music several times each minute as rollercoasters thrilled sugar-crazed passengers of all ages.

The girls grazed at the sticky puff of candy supported by the thin white paper cones they held. They watched the games being played, often by older boys attempting to show off and ultimately win something along the lines of a memento for their dates. The vendors played to the pride of these teenage boys, egging them to repeatedly pursue these feats of skill or strength following narrow failures and near misses. It went unsaid, but each girl imagined herself attending with a boy in subsequent years, Kathy reminding herself to enjoy the evening knowing that the other girls would indeed be escorted by boys a year from this very night.

Bea ventured a dollar and won a rainbow pen after one of her three Ping-Pong balls settled in a purple glass bowl amidst several dozen similarly shallow vessels. Not wanting to be burdened with a bulky prize, the girls left soon after devouring the colorful tufts of spun sugar. Bea nearly threw up after riding the roller coaster, and Lisa insisted upon touring the Haunted House, where boys were heard shrieking every bit as often as girls. Hailey urged the girls to pair up for the Ferris wheel, and they waited in line for the always-popular attraction. Boys their age and older admired Kathy's friends but paid her little heed as they walked past. It was something she had grown used to, forcing Kathy to once again remind herself how special she was, if only in the eyes of Grandma May. More often than not though lately, the thought had provided little solace.

As ten o'clock neared, the girls bought a hot cocoa and sat hip-to-hip on a small bench trying to decide on a final ride or game to play. They scanned the midway, knowing they had time for only one more activity before they must leave. Hailey pointed an ebony-tipped finger toward the fortune-teller's trailer, gleefully exclaiming, "Let's get our fortunes told!"

Lisa and Bea looked at one another and then at Hailey and Kathy before shrugging. "Why not?" they said in unison.

"Sounds fun. What do you say, Kathy?" Lisa asked.

Unconsciously mimicking her friends, Kathy shrugged her shoulders and raised a playful, if not dubious, eyebrow. "I'm game if you guys are," she said.

Madame Golivier – pronounced like the famous actor, but with a soft *g* in front – had just given up trying to reach her younger sister's cell phone. Lydia had promised to keep the device on her at all times but had proven unable to do that twice in the last week alone. So, Rhonda – Madame Golivier to her customers – was hopeful that Lydia had merely left her phone in the kitchen or bathroom counter while she was taking a bath or asleep in front of the television. It pained Rhonda to think of Lydia going into labor without her.

Mr. Robinson – he insisted upon being called *Mr.* – had reluctantly approved a two-day respite from her fortune-telling duties so that Rhonda could be by Lydia's side. The man was intimidated by anyone he suspected was brighter than he, and when she began to throw out phrases like *Family Leave Act* and *mandated excused absences*, he caved to her demands, clearly displeased at the implications and sharp eyebrow she raised while making her case. It was a far cry from their normal interaction, which consisted of him walking by her once a day and murmuring a hello, making visual contact not with her eyes but her ample cleavage instead. Tonight was the carnival's last night in Omaha. From here they would be heading to Lincoln for a three-day spell before heading south for the winter. Rhonda reasoned she would be able to catch up with the troupe if she drove hard and overnight, fueled by coffee and whatever stimulant she could glean from her friend Randy, who ran the merry-go-round. She only hoped her Tercel, with nearly two hundred thousand miles, was up to the task.

A hand on the trailer's squeaky handle caused Rhonda's eyes to dart reflexively toward the snub-nosed .38 she kept on the small shelf along the wall below her table. It was nearly ten, and the nearly forty-year old fortune-teller knew from experience how the clientele had a way of changing right around the turn of that particular hour. Bound by curfews, fresh-faced teens faded, retreating to their middle-class homes, replaced by older teens and delinquents, more often than not male, who roamed the midway emboldened by alcohol, or any of a number of other artificial forms of courage. Rhonda had never fired the small revolver after Randy had taken her to a quarry outside of Topeka, but she had long ago vowed she would not be cowed by drunken brutes who mistook her holding their palm to mean more than it did.

Relieved, Rhonda smiled at the four fresh faces that stepped into her trailer. There were two wooden chairs in front of the table where Rhonda sat facing the door. Two of the girls sat together on one of the chairs while a girl in a pink sweater sat on the small bench along the opposite wall, leaving the remaining chair for the rather buxom girl who was already wiping a palm on her pant leg in anticipation of having it read.

Like any other customer first setting foot in the darkened trailer, the girls looked around, smelling the incense, noticing the candles, old horror movie placards, and gypsy caravan photos designed to give the impression that Madame Golivier was of a long line of soothsayers. A crystal ball lay perched on a small cedar block in the middle of the dark blue felt-covered table. These young customers drank this in along with the black dress and transparent veil Golivier parted in order to see clearly that which might lay embedded in a palm for a buck, or within the presently opaque globe on the block for an additional dollar.

Madame Golivier smiled through beautiful and recently whitened teeth as she introduced herself to the girls. The one with the wiped palm pulled her sweatshirt sleeve up close to her elbow as if the reading of her palm might extend to veins in her forearm. The girl introduced herself as Hailey before referring to the two sharing the chair as being Lisa and Bea. The girl in the pink sweater was introduced as Kathy. Kathy smiled and held Golivier's eyes, unlike the chair sharers. It did not take a clairvoyant to see that Kathy was different, that it was more than just her pink sweater and choice of seating that set her apart from her companions. Golivier sensed there was more to the girl, but could not be certain as to what that *more* might involve.

After reading Hailey's palm – the girl seemed thrilled but hardly surprised to find that romance was just around the corner – Madame Golivier read Lisa and Bea's palms, finding romance and a splash of intrigue in both of their futures as well. Kathy stood after Bea was finished and put her hand on the trailer door.

"You're not going to have your palm read, Kathy?" Madame Golivier gently inquired.

Kathy smiled but shook her head. "Not today, thank you, ma'am" she said politely.

"You're not afraid, are you Kathy?" Golivier responded kindly.

"No. It's not that. It's just that we have to get going," Kathy said quietly.

Later, on the drive home from seeing her sister, Rhonda would wonder at what she had said next. "I'll read your palm for free, Kathy," she said demurely.

Lisa, Bea, and Hailey looked at Kathy, nodding. "Come on, Kath, we've still got time," Hailey urged.

Kathy ran her palm across the front of her sweater, uncertainly. The knitted fiber of the garment reminded her that she was dressed differently. It also reminded her of how badly she wanted to fit in, and how this year she had been more accepted than ever before. Getting along, sometimes meant going along, Grandma May had once insisted. "Okay. Sure," Kathy said, with a slight waver of trepidation evident only to the woman in black.

Hailey gave up her seat and stood over Kathy's shoulder as Madame Golivier gently grasped her wrist. The woman examined Kathy's open palm for a moment before smiling. Similar to before, Madame Golivier rendered a prophecy involving a hint of romance and the likelihood of a bright and wonderful future. And then, suddenly overcome with a gush of sentiment, likely inspired by her pending status as a first-time aunt, the carnival's oracle squeezed Kathy's hand with a bit of motherly compassion. "Your family loves you very much and feels you are quite special," she concluded.

Kathy smiled awkwardly but somewhat relieved as she stood up and pulled a dollar from her jeans pocket. The other girls were quiet, suppressing their giggles until they were well outside the trailer. "I thought she was going to hug you," Bea laughed.

"I think you were pretty smart, holding out," Hailey said.

"Yeah, I wish I'd thought of that," Lisa added.

"Why'd you give her the dollar?" Hailey asked, smacking her gum.

"Because she was right," Kathy returned confidently. "I am special."

"You go, girl!" Bea grinned.

"Anyone want a snow cone for the walk home?" Kathy said, as they neared a vendor selling scoops of multi-colored shaved ice.

"Sure," the others chimed in unison.

While Hailey and Lisa were getting their cones, Kathy grabbed a napkin and asked Bea if she could borrow the rainbow pen her friend had won earlier. They sat at a small round table, and Bea began to nibble at her cherry-flavored ice while Kathy hastily scribbled on the napkin.

"I'll be right back," Kathy said to Bea before trotting back to the fortune-teller's trailer. She almost grabbed the door handle but remembered the loud squeak and paused until she saw the small mail slot by the side of the door. After sliding the folded napkin through the slot, Kathy ran back to the table where her friends were all waiting for her.

"What was that all about?" Lisa asked.

"I just wrote her a little thank you note, was all," Kathy fibbed.

"Sure it wasn't another dollar you crammed in there?" Hailey smirked.

"I'm sure," Kathy returned smugly as they left the carnival grounds on their way home.

Two hours after the carnival lights dimmed and the grounds grew quiet, Rhonda had gotten the call from Lydia's husband, Dave. Within minutes she had been turning the ignition in the Tercel, and within hours she was holding her newborn niece, whom Dave proudly informed her was quite healthy despite being born a diminutive four pounds and eight ounces.

After two days that flew by all too quickly, Rhonda had found herself back in her car heading for Lincoln. It was in Lincoln that she found her trailer in its accustomed spot right next to the Mindbending Mirror display. And once inside the trailer she came across the napkin that Kathy had slipped through her mail slot just two days earlier. Rhonda picked it up and read the napkin.

Not bad for a buck. Wonder what I could charge???

Rhonda unfolded the napkin. *4 165 8 02* was scrawled inside.

Mulling over the note while she ate her breakfast and helped with set-up, Rhonda decided to call the number on the napkin, curious if the girl - Kathy had been her name – would answer. She had found herself thinking of Kathy on the late night drive to Lincoln, wondering how her newly born niece would fit into this world. Would she be on the inside like the three girls in sweatshirts or always just on the fringe like Kathy seemed to be? Rhonda couldn't imagine why Kathy would have left the number but was curious all the same. Before the sun began to set, Rhonda dialed the number after looking up the area code in a phone book Tiny Tina had lent her. To her disappointment the number was not serviceable.

The matter would have been laid to rest had Randy not come by for a nightcap following the dimming of lights and cessation of rides that same evening. The two had long been friends, and the weathered merry-go-round operator had looked forward to catching up, hearing about Rhonda's sister and newborn niece. Randy sat at her table while Rhonda searched for a bottle of gin, filling him in on the details while she looked through various cabinets.

"Is this what your niece weighed?" Randy asked, picking up the napkin Kathy had left.

Rhonda glanced over her shoulder. "No, that's just some number a customer left," she said, at last spying the bottle of gin. "I tried it, but the number's disconnected," Rhonda continued as Randy studied the napkin.

"So the baby didn't weigh 4 lbs 8 oz?" Randy queried, looking at the *4 l65 8 02*, Kathy had scrawled in a hand that her friends often found difficult to transcribe.

Closely Knit

Late spring and all that recommends it is in plain view for any who care to observe both flora and fauna this first day of June. Few, however, are inclined to notice as most of the town's population has made its way to the Clare Union High School football stadium, which isn't really much of a stadium, but referring to it as such gives many in the community a sense of pride, just the same. Families mill through the parking lot, clutching sack lunches and drinks, fathers with a hand on the shoulders of their sons, mothers clutching their children's hands regardless of age, the youth allowing it on this day, despite many feeling too old for such sentiment. Quite a few grandparents have made the trip out of curiosity or nostalgia, although they no longer participate directly in the day's activities. There is a subdued murmur as families fill in the home team bleachers that are no more comfortable than anyone remembers them being during football season, which ended with a first round playoff loss to the Hillsboro Titans the previous November. Many have brought pillows or even cushions with aluminum backings to offer lumbar support for the regular sports fan.

Many are the towns and communities where it is said casually that everyone knows everyone. Such towns often feature communication networks that involve clotheslines, four – not five – foot backyard fences, barber shops, book clubs, quiet pubs, and granges where wedding receptions, town meetings, and bingo nights swirl around one another in accommodative fashion most months of the year. And while there can certainly be drawbacks to everyone knowing everyone else's business, for the most part, these towns tend to engender a real sense of community. Most of the residents of Clare Iowa regard themselves as *truly* part of such a town, suspecting with good reason that their community is far more closely knit than most, where *everyone knows everyone* is more often than not merely a figure of speech.

Mayor Morgan Steele approaches a modest lectern and taps the microphone repeatedly, causing people to cover their ears at the resulting cacophony. He evidently finds humor in this, and a broad smile breaks across his plump and sagging face. A gust of wind blows the pompous top hat he wears from his head exposing his nearly bald pate, and snickers break across the stands evening the score as he stoops to retrieve the hat before it blows off of the same makeshift platform that supported the crowning of last November's Homecoming Queen, Angela Taylor. Also on stage is the lovely Mrs. Pickering who is seated primly at a folding table featuring the large, wire-caged orb borrowed from the Bingo committee at the grange. Mrs. Pickering is tucking her long skirt under her thighs so that a similar gust of wind doesn't expose those in the stands to underwear her husband refers to as *grannies.*

A small plastic grocery sack skims along the surface of the football field behind the stage like solitary tumbleweed, and more eyes than not follow it before Mayor Steele requests that everyone rise for the Pledge of Allegiance. Men, women, and children face the flag above the north end zone, but many eyes are distracted, wavering between the flag blowing gloriously in the breeze and the wire cage in front of Mrs. Pickering.

There is an unmistakable tension in the air, but a

panoramic scan of the audience reveals vastly different emotions countenanced on the faces of those in the stands. Some are joyous, eagerly anticipating the events that will follow the opening ceremonies; while some are clearly sad and more than a bit distraught; while still others look to be a curious mix of emotions. The children in particular, appear to be anxious, swallowing with tight throats, squeezing the parental hands they hold and scanning the stands around them with a bit of trepidation and uncertainty, if not a dash of hopefulness.

When all are seated following the Pledge of Allegiance, it is so quiet that the flag's flapping can be heard from every seat. Mayor Steele takes his time reviewing the rules and protocol, reveling in the importance of the role he plays with the zeal of an inebriated game show host, feeling the need to dress up the occasion as if the event itself were not captivating enough. Several community members wish for another gust that would take his hat away. More than one hormone-inspired teen thinks of what that same gust could reveal under Mrs. Pickering's skirt. Finally, at the conclusion of the rules and procedural review, Mayor Steele requests that all the children between the ages of four and seventeen make their way down to the field where they line up shoulder to shoulder in two lines that extend from nearly one end zone to the other. The mayor announces that a total of two hundred and seventy-three children will participate this year, up eleven from last year, he notes with pride.

Allowed to stand as they like, many of the children are holding hands, most faces adorned with a stiff upper lip, looking into the stands as if facing a firing squad. Mayor Steele, who currently has two daughters, gives them both a smile before once again facing the stands, a look of gravity on his face. He clears his throat and asks Mrs. Pickering to begin turning the wheel. She begins to do so, and it is clear that the big cage is not as easy to turn as it might look, due to the collective weight of its contents. But Mrs. P gradually builds up some momentum, and the thing soon takes on a life of its own. Mayor Steele holds up his hand, and Mrs. Pickering applies the brake to the wheel causing all the shiny, white plastic discs inside to tumble in abandonment of centrifugal force. Pausing for dramatic effect, Mayor Steele plucks the microphone from the podium and reminds his audience that each and every one of the children's names is, in fact, in the cage because he has personally seen to it not once but twice.

So intent are the adults in the stands to proceed that no one bothers to murmur or even roll their eyes at this needless attempt to add to a level of suspense that is already painfully palpable throughout the stadium. Satisfied he has achieved this end, Mayor Steele reaches into the wire basket while directing his eyes in the opposite direction in a vaudevillian attempt to convey a demeanor of absolute integrity.

"Jerold and Mary Allen, you are first on the list. Would you be so kind as to stand so that all the children can see you?" Steele scans the crowd.

A couple slowly stands on one end of the stadium half way up the bleachers. All eyes are fixed on this couple, including those of the two young children that left their laps to stand opposite them on the field in hopes of maintaining eye contact with Jerold and Mary during the proceedings.

The Mayor plucks a disc from the nearly three hundred that are pooled on the bottom of the stationary cage. He brings it to his face and squints with exaggeration before reaching into his pocket in a clearly premeditated and orchestrated fashion for his glasses. He obviously intends to provide comic relief, but no one laughs, and more than a few can recollect him having pulled the same flat stunt last year and possibly even the year before that.

"Allison Crenshaw," Mayor Steele enunciates with exaggerated diction into the microphone. He had considered turning the mic off before announcing the first name but opted against it after his first gag failed to produce the laughter he'd sought. A small blonde girl in a yellow dress steps forth at hearing her name. She immediately glances over her shoulder at the young girl who had been sitting on Mary Allen's lap before the Pledge. The young girl gives Allison Crenshaw a tight-lipped smile and barely perceptible nod of encouragement at which Allison brightens noticeably before walking up the stadium stairs in the direction of the Allens.

"If memory serves me," the Mayor continues, peeking at the list on the podium, "the Allens surrendered not one, but two children this year." He then proceeds to withdraw a second disc from the cage. "Mathew Broder, you are to be the Allen's second child for the entirety of the next year."

At this, a rather surly looking teen in need of a haircut steps forth with shoulders slouching. His gait, as he follows Allison Crenshaw's route toward the Allens, suggests disinterest, but his heart is pounding as wildly as any other. By the time Mathew Broder reaches his new family Mayor Steele has created two more brand new families. The Allens, Andersons, and Atwells behind them are technically free to leave now, but no one ever does so at this juncture. It would not look well to leave before seeing where former children are placed, not to mention those they'd actually birthed.

Naysayers and detractors can be found in abundance in the towns and communities surrounding Clare. Some of Clare's own citizens disapprove of the practice, although most of the disbelievers move away when they are old enough to venture forth on their own. This principle and methodology of upbringing was actually the impetus for the founding of Clare, as many of the former residents of nearby Hillsboro grew frustrated with the crime, graffiti, neglect, and general apathy that flourished within the ranks of that town's youth, foreboding a level of future societal decay that the older generation deemed unacceptable. Long ago, several dozen families decided to leave Hillsboro and the town's traditional practice of childrearing, choosing to relocate in the small hamlet of St. Clare, which they promptly shortened to simply Clare.

Although eventually credited to one politician or another, the notion that it takes a village to raise a child was more or less originated hundreds of years ago and simply taken to heart by the people of Clare upon deciding how best to both edify and codify their youth. What they came up with was a system whereby parents who gave birth to a child would submit their biological progeny - after the child turned four - to the lottery system we see employed today. The child would keep its original surname, but become a part of a different family each year for roughly thirteen years before being reunited with his or her biological parents for their senior year of high school. In theory, the adolescent by this time would have been exposed to a diverse upbringing including a variety of cuisine, travel, religious concepts, values, races, political views, socio-economic levels, and parenting skills with which to employ when or if the time came for them to have children of their own.

The citizens of Clare believe that it has made for a community in which everyone has a vested interest in the well-being of everyone else's children, a community where any given adult would be free to chastise a youth for littering or cursing should the need arise. Relative to the outlying towns and communities, the citizens of Clare boast of cleaner schools, nearly perfect attendance at parent conferences, higher grades on average, and fewer disciplinary issues - at least after things completely settle down to the new normal, usually about the middle of each October.

Of course, there are drawbacks, as the people of Clare readily – and their detractors *eagerly* – acknowledge. For obvious reasons, the young people of Clare are not allowed to date until their senior year and then only to children they've not been siblings to, biologically or otherwise. While the enforcement of this rule has not always been easy, the townspeople are quick to point out a nearly nonexistent level of sexually transmitted disease or teen pregnancy in their community. Failure to mention the occasional suicide or runaway would be remiss, but the rate of each is actually quite in line with national averages.

While rare, the occasional divorce is usually granted by the courts the day before the lottery or draft as some call it. Divorced individuals are ineligible and must begin anew if they remarry; that is to say, any of their biological children go to the surplus list to be granted to families that apply for eligibility after any barren couples are accommodated.

Needless to say, there is a period of adjustment

as each summer begins, with families acclimating, guidelines and expectations issued, and a natural sadness felt by both parents and children for their families of the previous year. By the time most children have participated in three or four families they have proven themselves to be quite adaptable. The summer is thought to be a good time for bonding, and after a family vacation or two most children have already begun to assimilate. By the time school starts in the fall the vast majority of families are in a routine and reasonably well adjusted. Counseling exists for families or individuals that need additional help with the transition.

Schools are, no doubt, a big part of what makes the transitions as smooth and successful as they usually are. Teachers tailor adaptation lessons in the fall as well as preparing the younger students for the upcoming change as the school year approaches an end. Camaraderie in Clare is exceptional as the children experience endearment with a great many students over the years. It goes a long way in explaining why so few actually choose to leave the community upon graduating. Most who go on to universities come back to Clare to settle, if not right away.

Other factors that seem to help add to the sense of community are the monthly Clare Community Mixers, or CCMs that all are encouraged to attend. July is a carnival; August features the county fair; September is a Back-to-School Bonanza featuring raffles, cakewalks, bingo, and dunk tanks; a huge costume party marks Halloween; a Thanksgiving Parade is quite well attended in late November; December features the very popular Christmas Concert in the high school gym followed by a party/dance; January is Bingo Night (with fantastic donated prizes!); February is a Valentines dance/party; March is the Founders Day potluck; April is the all-town Easter Egg hunt; May brings the big auction which always follows a pancake feed; and June, of course, is Stadium Day where the new familial assignments are made, followed by a huge picnic on the football field.

There is a good deal of shifting done on the bleacher seats as Mayor Steele nears the end of the alphabet, due not only to the less than comfortable seating but to hunger as well, since it is now nearing noon. The Uptons, Yates, Wilsons, and Wolfes are studying the nearly dozen youth that remain on the field, a process of elimination allowing them to roughly surmise who they will be eating with and taking home following the picnic.

As the newly formed families make their way down to the field with blankets, lunch sacks, and drinks it is evident there is a good deal of optimism and love in the stadium; for most of the citizens of Clare greatly prefer their method of upbringing to the traditional method that saw their ancestors raised in institutions, as is still practiced in nearby Hillsboro.

Sounds Familiar

Neil Green found that most people, upon learning that he was a middle-school teacher, reacted with similar responses. Some would shake their head in uncertainty, telling him, *I don't know how you do it.* Others, while shaking their heads, would simply mutter, *Kids these days.* Still others, would ask if he was a glutton for punishment. But Neil, most definitely not a glutton for punishment, *did* know how he did it and often found himself thinking, *Parents these days*.

After serving nearly a full tour in Afghanistan, Neil knew punishment, and teaching was anything but. In fact, in the five years Neil had been teaching, he had experienced nothing but reward. The corny cards that echoed sentiments along the lines of *teaching touches lives forever,* and *the influence of a good teacher never ends*, were, in fact, largely true, Neil concluded, if one was able to establish a rapport with the young charges under their tutelage.

Forgoing the staff room to eat at the cramped cafeteria tables with his students, playing football and foursquare at recess, and attending their games on weekends, all served to ingratiate Neil to both parents and students alike. Neil enjoyed seeing his students as they cut their teeth gaining a sense of humor. At the end of the year he played a recording of them reading aloud for the first time in his class, back in September. The pride that showed in their faces as they realized how much they had improved and how far they had come was but one of the many intangible rewards.

For Neil, teaching was the perfect profession - practical, rewarding, and peaceful. Peaceful in a way that Neil had not known prior to entering the profession. It was also very different from anything he had ever tried before. Growing up in a family imbued with patriotic spirit, Neil had originally attempted to follow in his father and grandfather's footsteps by enlisting in the military.

Basic training had gone well. But a month after finding his unit stationed in Kandahar, the buzzing sounds that had plagued him from time to time in his youth became bothersome. The sound, both like bees buzzing and a harsh grating, became worse with each day. Neil became embarrassed, thinking the sound was all in his head as it subsided on the long jeep ride to a nearby province where the Army had a specialist. There was hardly any sound at all as the doctor looked in his ears, asked him questions, and gave him a prescription for what Neil realized was anxiety.

The sound ramped up in volume and intensity as the jeep neared the barracks on the ride home from the clinic. Neil covered his ears and moved his jaw from side to side, hoping the sound would go away. Despite being well liked and affable, Neil found that the noise was less intense when he was by himself. It was too hot to run and too dangerous to go far, but Neil began taking walks by himself in the early morning before breakfast was served. These brief sojourns, an effort to enjoy a temporary respite from the increasingly uncomfortable noise. As the weeks and months passed the walks were less and less effective in keeping the noise at bay. The intensity of the noise became simply unbearable when Neil was in the midst of his unit. Prolonged bouts left him shaking like a heroin addict in need of a fix.

In an effort to separate himself from the noise

which he now associated with his unit, Neil began volunteering to take point as the unit caravanned in jeeps, Humvees, and supply trucks along the barren highways and roads. The men, with whom Neil had enjoyed camaraderie following basic training, now began to see him as something of a lone wolf.

Some questioned his motives. What was he trying to prove? Was he seeking a medical release at the risk of life and limb? Was he suicidal? Was their friend close to snapping, endangering their lives as well? It was rare to find a volunteer to ride in front due to the IEDs and roadside bomb blasts that had numbed the American public with daily headlines for several years now.

Neil had, in fact, determined that being sent home was going to be his only salvation. His quality of sleep deteriorating daily, Neil feared he would crack up and be sent home with a Section Eight discharge, which he would carry around for the rest of his life both at home and in the workplace. Growing up in a family with a legacy of military service, this was not an option. A self-inflicted wound would be easy to recognize and medical personnel were trained to look for such injuries. Neil would need to be legitimately injured or killed in order to be sent home. So dire had become the problem, that Neil was willing to take his chances driving point.

Strangely enough, the roadside bomb that turned his vehicle on its side blew out Neil's eardrums in addition to killing the soldier in the passenger seat. The cacophony in Neil's head as he lay in the hospital awaiting to get in a transport jet bound for the states, was somewhat muted and altogether different from that to which he had grown accustomed.

Several months later, having recovered his hearing after being honorably discharged, Neil decided to enroll in his local police academy. While not exactly military, this certainly pleased his father, who liked to boast of his son, the Purple Heart recipient. The academy promoted some of the same camaraderie that Neil had enjoyed during basic training, and he thrived on the thought of having left the debilitating noise behind.

Neil Green flew through the twelve-week program with flying colors and soon found himself in a squad room with two dozen other officers. The sound that had so debilitated Neil in Afghanistan had abated for the most part. From time to time it would crop up for short stints, but it was far less intense and usually only lasted a few minutes.

Patrolman Tom Parker had been assigned to showing Neil the ropes, and the two headed out to patrol the beat Tom had known for the better part of five years. Neil felt like a little kid when he heard himself ask if Tom had ever had to shoot anyone.

Tom just chuckled and said, "Some guys may be embarrassed to say they've never had to draw their weapon. Me? I'm grateful. I'd like to retire being able to say that. What about you? Sarge said you were in Afghanistan."

"No. I fired a few mortars once, but I was in communications. Carried the same Glock we are now, but never fired it other than the range," Neil answered amiably.

A few weeks later Neil found himself partnered with officer Jim Rizzo, who jovially informed Neil that Tom, "musta met the Monday Morning Monster." Neil must have looked puzzled because the man winked and whispered, "hangover," in an effort to clarify.

"I'm feeling that way, and I didn't have anything to drink," Neil commented, rubbing his temple in an effort to thwart the modest buzzing that had begun in his head.

As their patrol car rolled out of the precinct parking lot, Rizzo asked Neil, "You ready to put holes in bad people if the need arises?"

Neil wasn't sure if Rizzo was kidding, but felt he was being tested all the same. "You ever seen the need arise?" He asked genially.

"Once or twice," Rizzo responded, trying to sound casual.

The drive home from the station brought almost instant relief to Neil, who realized the day had featured his longest bout with the buzzing, grating noise since he had left Kandahar. It was at a stop sign a mile from home that Neil realized the cause of the noise.

As a child, the single most intense bout with the noise had taken place on a trip to Disneyland. His father had left the main highway in an attempt to cut forty miles off the AAA estimated mileage total on their Triptik. His mother had grown frustrated and worried, as their reunion with the main highway had failed to materialize. Neil's father had pulled into a small rest area opposite a huge, concrete, fenced facility. Together, his mother and father began bickering and pointing as they poured over the map. The noise in Neil's head began to mount, growing by the minute. He placed his hands over his ears in an effort to stop the noise, groaning lightly as he did.

Neil's mother had sharply told him to be patient. The groaning continued from the back seat causing her to turn around. Neil was red-faced and crying as he began to scream, "Make it stop! Make the noise stop." Despite her efforts to soothe the boy,

Neil's mother was unable to keep her son from screaming. She began to insist they find a hospital. Neil's father, now quite flustered, uttered a curse and gunned the van out of the rest area where a group of bikers sat on a picnic bench smoking cigarettes.

"Pull in here," Neil's mother implored, pointing to the large facility. "Maybe someone here can tell us how to get to a hospital."

"Like hell," Neil's father responded. "See that razor wire, dear? I'm not going to ask directions at a state prison."

As the van drove away from correctional facility, Neil began to calm until the noise was no longer heard inside his head. His mother, thinking he was hungry, insisted that her son eat a granola bar in order to stop his shaking. This seemed to do the trick, as the shaking decreased with each mile the van distanced itself from the facility that warehoused some of the most hardened killers in the country.

Neil confirmed his theory after his shift ended the next day, as he loitered around the briefing, staff, and locker rooms. The noise, which was barely perceptible outside the precinct station, became louder as he entered and definitely more amplified and pronounced in the immediate presence of some officers. Other officers, like Tom Parker, seemingly had no effect on the sound being emitted in Neil's head. A few casual questions placed here and there among his fellow officers combined with some Internet research allowed Neil Green to conclude that the noise inside his head was caused by the presence of an individual who had taken at least one human life.

It was for this reason that Neil was so disturbed early one September morning to find that the long dormant noise had returned as he greeted his new class of nervous sixth-graders.

The Right Call

Having wished many times for the opportunity to meet any number of historical figures, Randall Walker found himself facing just such an opportunity after a brief conversation with an impeccably dressed man on a midtown bus ride, in which the man somehow transported them both from the noisy, crowded diesel into a most magnificent library featuring infinite and ideal reading for a professor of American history such as Randall. The man was now seated, hands clasped, across from Randall at a massive, lengthy, and perfectly polished oak table. Randall struggled to make sense of the scenic transformation and found his senses overloaded with stimuli beyond all but his wildest imagination.

On the one hand, the room was simply magnificent, with parallel oak-encased walls nearly twenty feet in height, packed with thick historical volumes ordered chronologically and appearing to cover every era of history since the beginning of time. An adjacent wall featured a river rock fireplace so massive that the stones were actually basketball-sized boulders. Round six-foot lengths of log were burning lustily, providing both warmth and atmosphere. The remaining partition consisted of a long pony wall of additional volumes nearing four feet in height. Above the shelf was one giant triangular pane of spotless glass affording a seemingly limitless view, although all Randall could discern were clouds.

On the other hand, the vaguely familiar looking man seated in front of Randall was wearing a tweed sport coat Randall could remember admiring in a mail-order catalogue just last week. He was saying something, and Randall had to focus on the man's words, as if the stimuli provided by the magnificent room were draining his attentive resources. "Would you like more time to consider your decision?" the man asked pleasantly.

"My decision?" Randall rasped.

"Yes. On the bus, you said you were a professor of American history, and I asked if you would like to meet anyone in particular," the man explained reasonably. "You said, 'Yes, but they're all dead.' And I asked you who you'd want to meet if their demise proved to be no obstacle."

Randall swallowed and looked around the room again, still unsure of his bearings. His throat felt dry, and Randall noticed the man was gesturing to a tall, clear glass of water at Randall's elbow. Randall took the glass and held it up. The water was perfectly clear, and he could see the man through the water, distorted not in the least. Randall sipped the water and thought about replacing the glass on the table but didn't because there hadn't been a coaster, and he didn't want to mar the flawlessly polished table by leaving a ring. But glancing down he noticed there was now a coaster where but a moment before there had been none.

"You're telling me," Randall paused to gather himself. "You're telling me I can meet anyone from any period of history?"

"I had presumed because of your station that you would be interested in an American. But yes, you name the individual, and they'll come through those doors within moments," the man said agreeably, gesturing to the double oak door entrance in the midst of the book-lined wall behind Randall, who suddenly couldn't recall entering the room at all.

"Jesus," Randall muttered.

"That I can't do," the man grimaced slightly. "Technically not mortal the way we see it. Anyone else, you name it."

"No. I meant. Never mind." Randall placed the glass on the coaster and leaned back. "So if I tell you I want to meet Abe Lincoln, he'll just walk through that door?"

The man smiled. "All seventy-six inches of him."

"Robert E. Lee?"

"Just give me the word," the man nodded.

Randall's head began to swim with historical figures and possibilities. "Genghis Khan?"

"In the flesh."

While not ordinarily given to believing preposterous claims made by strangers aboard public transportation, Randall had to admit that just moments ago he was on the verge of dozing while heading home after giving back-to-back lectures on causes leading to the Great Depression. He looked around the room once more and allowed himself to believe that maybe, just maybe this stranger could deliver on such a promise. If so, the possibilities were limitless.

"Would you like a few moments to yourself, while you decide?" The man asked, getting up from the table. "Take your time. Make yourself at home. Just rap on the table when you're ready."

Randall willed himself to nod. "Thank you," he muttered to the man who was now walking through the doors, closing them both quietly behind him.

Sophocles, Aristotle, Cleopatra, Washington, Michelangelo, Caesar, Joan of Arc, King Henry VIII - *Elizabeth* for that matter, Lincoln, Shakespeare, Tubman, Churchill; any one of which he could have summoned to this very table if he willed it. It was too amazing to even contemplate, and yet here he was, doing just that. So many brilliant minds, so much courage, perseverance, wisdom, and fortitude from which to choose: it was positively mindboggling. Before long, Randall realized he must adopt some semblance of a process of elimination. No sooner had he made this determination than he found a legal pad and silver ballpoint pen on the table next to his water glass.

Every time he was able to eliminate a figure, two more possibilities popped into his mind. It was worse than combating Hydra. The Thomases alone were mind boggling with Jefferson, Aquinas, Hobbes, and Edison leaping to the forefront. Capricious or whimsical elimination would not do. Randall realized he must have a standard-bearer or two, and strike down candidates relative to how they compared with his personal heroes. Within minutes he had the list down to three, two of them Americans and the third a Brit; as one by one he painstakingly excised all other names from the legal pad.

Washington, Lincoln, and Churchill survived the cut because Randall had studied all three in great detail and admired their courage and integrity beyond words. All three were gifted leaders and powerful speakers. Churchill and Lincoln were intellectual giants, while Washington was given to sacrifice like few others. A slew of questions came to mind for each - so many things Randall would love to ask and learn. Strategy, considerations, regrets, unrealized objectives - once again, Randall wouldn't know where to begin. Did they waver in their hearts when times were bleak and dire, despite the brave fronts they put on for the countless masses looking to them for leadership?

Despite his great admiration and appreciation for the British Bulldog, Randall, with great reluctance, eliminated Churchill from contention. The patriotic professor had written a thesis and dissertation on the first and sixteenth presidents, respectively. Both giants had faced the elimination of their great nation and had taken enormous personal risks. Randall knew he could not lose in choosing either man.

In deciding, Randall broke from his reverie. He looked at his watch and found it had stopped, probably at the time he had left the bus, Randall reasoned. About to knock on the table, Randall took one last look about the library. A large silver tray to the right of the massive fireplace held several tumblers surrounding crystal decanters of what looked to be a number of fine spirits. Remembering the man's words *make yourself at home*, Randall walked to the tray and helped himself to a finger and a half of what smelled like well-aged scotch. He walked the length of the room toward the window, admiring the leather bound volumes, many of which he had read, a few he had even authored.

Looking out the window onto a carpet of clouds caused Randall to momentarily ponder the altitude in which he found himself. Randall noticed a long corridor lined with what appeared to be blooming cherry trees consistent with the early May afternoon. Cherry trees made him smile as he recalled his choice. *Was this heaven?* Randall mused. He drank the scotch, savoring the taste as it ran over his tongue and decided that it was time.

Rapping his knuckles gently on the table brought the man back, right on queue as promised. Randall sat down again following the man's lead. "You've made your decision, I take it?" the man inquired gently.

"I'm ready," Randall said earnestly before whispering the name of his selection solemnly across the table.

No sooner had the man nodded in affirmation than the clouds that had canvassed the scenery beyond the window moved through the giant pane and into the room, swirling and misty. The visibility in the library became so limited that Randall could not see the hand he held to his face. He heard the oak doors open and close a moment later, and while he couldn't hear footsteps he could sense another presence in the room and before long at the table. Despite the comfortable temperature, Randall felt a chill of excitement as the mist began to abate.

Before long he could make out the silhouette across the table, and a moment later he could see white hair pulled back. Instinctively, Randall reached for the gnarled hands on the table in front of him. "Mother, I've missed you so much."

Brothers With a Capital Bee

When I first read about the procedure my brother discovered being responsible for saving upwards of twenty-five thousand lives a year, I must admit, I felt a perverse sense of having contributed to the medical community myself, if only indirectly. Not that I ever went to medical school or even spent time in a hospital outside of having my appendix removed and visiting our father a few times after his first heart attack. No, I never even completed a first aid course after they started including CPR, undone by the thought of mouthing Annie's greying lips, still wet from rubbing alcohol after the obese smoker I was partnered with got done nearly impregnating her. Instead, I ended up running to words, stringing them together in enough sentences, paragraphs, pages, and chapters to pass as novels portraying crime in a way that allowed readers to rubberneck without actually slowing traffic. Voyeurship for the warped, I called it – this service I rendered to my readers - usually the type with cigarette burns between their index and middle fingers due to a nearly comatose absorption with the macabre. A hack was what the critics called me, not altogether unfairly, I might add. Hell, sell enough copies and who gives a rat's ass what they call you.

So here's the irony: my brother, David, you know, the one who is responsible for saving twenty-five thousand lives a year – that's a million over the next forty years, by the way - in addition to those he saves working as a surgeon fifty hours a week, took home about a third of what I pulled in last year. I write about dismembering *fictitious* people, and he actually fixes and sews up *real* people, and *I* make the big bucks. How sick is that? Of course, David doesn't really care about money, so long as his wife and kids are happy. Good thing too – I asked him once about the malpractice insurance he's forced to buy – no wonder these docs want a hundred bucks to put a band aid on your ass or slip you an aspirin. Anyway, he literally *gave* this miraculous procedure to the medical community. Figured it out as an intern while watching a transplant, tried it on a cadaver before running it by the senior surgeon or whoever at his hospital. Guy writes an article about it, giving my brother all the credit of a freaking footnote. My brother doesn't get a dime, and the damn procedure's not even named after him. And he doesn't even give a damn; he tells me it doesn't matter who gets credit so long as lives are saved. He says he's acknowledged within the medical community, and that's good enough for him.

I love the kid. I really do. But you've got to wonder what goes on in his head sometimes. Like the time we were kids, and he tried to save the possum I shot going through our trash. David is trying to take a .22 shell out of this thing that's bleeding profusely, trying to scratch the hell out of him, and probably rabid. The serial killers I write about almost invariably start out torturing small animals, and here my brother is trying to save the furry little devils. I think we all knew he was going to be a doctor even before that, though. He'd memorized the names of all the bones and muscles in the human body- 'lotta Latin goobledegook' according to our father – by the time he was in middle school; a time when most guys were only interested in breasts and thighs - whether on women or poultry.

I don't mean to sound like I'm down on David.

Like I said, I love the kid. And who am I to question how his life turned out anyway? He's been married to the same smart gorgeous gal for nearly twenty years now on top of having two beautiful razor-sharp kiddos. Believe it or not, their yard is actually enclosed by a white picket fence. Me, I've been divorced three times and pay more than David makes in alimony and child support. So again, who am I to judge David? And besides, he loves me, never acknowledges my faults, and never judges me. The guy still calls and asks for my advice whenever he purchases a car. He faithfully reads each book I churn out, asking me to sign a copy before he puts it on a special shelf in his library devoted exclusively to my drivel. When I checked myself in for the appendix, he rushed down to see me and made sure I got the best surgeon on call that day. Who's there when I come out of it? David's there with his wife and kids. I thought I was on the set with Ward and June until the anesthesia wore off. I don't even think I mentioned the appendix to my kids, who only call when tuition is due.

Sometimes I think David was adopted. Then I have to remind myself that I was at the hospital the day he was born. The kid had lungs; I'll give him that. He cried all the way home and for the next week, and the weeks after that. Our parents had tried to build up what a big help I was going to be as a big brother and all. You know, the usual crap adults pull when they're trying to be sensitive to the older kid having their nose out of joint when the new baby starts sucking all the air out of the room, getting all the attention that used to go to big brother. We painted my bedroom a color I was allowed to choose, but that was little solace considering I was to share the room until we moved to a bigger house three and a half years later.

I suppose there was some of that natural resentment, but what I really remember is the piercing, nonstop crying. Our mother explained how David was just colicky, nothing like the eating, sleeping and pooping little fellow I'd been, she said. Dad found extra hours and took additional shifts when guys called in sick – anything to get out of the house and away from David the Decibel. I couldn't blame him, but at eight I couldn't pick up and leave when I felt like it. I can remember trying to get away with a Hardy Boys novel, trying to find any place in the house where I couldn't hear the crying. I tried plugging my ears with bits of paper that resulted in earaches shortly after my next bath. Finally, I went out to the garage and read with a flashlight while listening to mice eat kibble in our garbage can.

At night I would lay in my bed waiting for David to fall asleep, covering myself with pillows in an effort to block the noise. I'd feel myself get all tense, as anger and a lack of sleep combined to make me see red. Then, when I thought he'd never stop, David would wind down, allowing me to slowly do the same as we each settled into a light sleep. Only to be awakened again with a shrill scream followed by another hour of crying! Awakening in this fashion felt like having a heart attack, not to mention disrupting dreams that were often inspired by seeing the teenage girl next door sunning herself without a top. Often, my mother would come in, take David, and walk him around the house, chortling and comforting the little bastard fruitlessly. Soon she gave up and began to allow him to cry it out after burping him repeatedly.

One such night, a few days after Christmas, I'd

had enough and taken my pillow and blankets into the living room where I camped out on the couch. The crying continued, and I got madder and madder as the couch caused me to itch uncontrollably. My mother had given it her best shot and returned to her bedroom. My father was working the night shift and wouldn't be home until the early morning. I lay there, recalling my parents talking one day in the car when they thought I was asleep. They spoke of my mother's aunt losing a child to Sudden Infant Death Syndrome many years ago. They said doctors couldn't explain the phenomenon to this day.

The crying continued, and I could take it no longer. I rose from the couch and took my pillow into David's and my room where I stood over him as moonlight streamed across his red puckered face. I was lowering the pillow to his face when my foot jolted with pain. I hopped about the floor and flipped on the light as David stopped screaming. On the floor, in the middle of winter mind you, was a crushed honeybee.

The colic left my brother that night and never returned. I'll never be able to explain the bee, but I'll be forever grateful it was there. And while they don't know it, so should twenty-five thousand others - per annum.

Quarterlies

Despite local forecasts insisting that Tillamook would only get close, the temperature *had* dipped below freezing in the early hours of the morning. The possibility of ice never occurred to the young woman who always garaged her car in an effort to ward off the corrosive effects of sea air. It was not until the vehicle was spinning sideway and out of control that ice entered her mind as a possible culprit. This notion was surely among the last of her thoughts as the car slammed into the massive fir tree that bore only a reflective yellow sign with an arrow warning of the sharp curve in the road.

The squeaking noise in front of her house a moment earlier gave Helen a fair idea as to who was knocking at her door. If she thought it was anyone else she might have ignored the gentle rapping. But the woman who delivered her mail was kind and caring when she could have easily brought the mail back to the post office deeming it undeliverable. Helen dropped the damp washcloth that had straddled her forehead for the past hour into the sink and brushed several stray locks of hair behind her ears before opening the door.

The mail carrier smiled gently and without judgment, her blue latex-gloved hand full of mail, mostly the junk variety. Helen smiled sheepishly, her eyes flitting from the carrier's to the mail in the woman's hand. "I'm sorry. I keep forgetting." Helen took the mail with both hands. "Mostly bills anyway," she continued, as if this explained why she regularly failed to retrieve her mail from the box at the end of her driveway until it became so full that no more could be packed inside the cylinder bearing her name.

"I think I saw a gardening magazine in there," the woman offered, her voice attempting a measure of optimism.

"Thank you so much. I'm sorry to put you to the trouble. I'll put a note on the fridge reminding me. You shouldn't have to do this," Helen stammered, embarrassed.

The woman smiled sadly. "It's no trouble." It occurred to Helen that this woman knew of her loss and pitied her. A trace of anger welled momentarily within her; short-lived, as it was no match for the abundance of self-pity that had made her its host for better than six months now.

Helen wondered if the mail carrier knew the extent of Helen's loss. Had the woman heard that Helen had lost her only child, or did the woman also know that in addition to losing her son she had also lost her husband, although to far less tragic circumstances? Helen looked toward the refrigerator, possibly even with the intention of writing a reminder on it, but once she saw the small white dry-erase board, smudged with black ink around the edges, remnants of words obliterated by a small palm in order to make room for a single word, her intent vaporized. The sole word dominating the rectangular board read, T R A I N. A not-so-subtle reminder of what Robbie had wanted for his birthday, had wanted since seeing *Thomas the Train* on television over at his grandparent's house a year ago.

It occurred to Helen that she was unlikely to ever see these grandparents again. *And why should she?* They were Scott's parents, and if she were unlikely to see Scott again, what circumstances would have her seeing his parents? None that she could foresee. Scott had left less than three months after the accident, no doubt blaming himself for what had happened to Robbie. Helen had been unable to convince her husband that he was not to blame. After all, how could he have known that a freak gust of wind would come up, blowing a folding chair *unsecured* from the top of a parked motor home and onto the skull of one of sixty children walking amidst a dozen chaperones through a parking lot at the Oregon Museum of Science and Industry? *One in sixty?* That didn't even begin to depict the odds of such a happening.

Scott had beaten himself up, insisting that he shouldn't have sent Robbie to school that day, the boy still weak from battling a cold over the weekend. Robbie's temperature had returned to normal, his nose no longer running, Scott declared. Helen, who had been at her sister's, had tried to reassure Scott, telling him she too would have sent Robbie to school that day. *Wouldn't she?* At any rate, nothing Helen could say or do served to quell the guilt and anxiety Scott felt. Late one afternoon coming in from a solitary walk, prepared to start cooking dinner, *defrosting lasagna actually*, Helen had found Scott packing several cardboard boxes on their bed. He insisted he was leaving her everything, wouldn't even take their matching luggage, just wanted to be away from this house, these picture-filled walls - every room a multitude of memories.

Still not comprehending what was happening, Helen, through tears, had attempted to hold her husband, insisting that it was all right if he wanted to move; they could put the house up for sale immediately. Scott had peeled her rigid hands from his wrinkled shirt. It was the last time he would look at her directly, in the eyes, explaining that she was part of Robbie, that looking in her eyes was seeing him, the son he had sent to school despite a voice from within telling him to keep Robbie home.

The cabinet was nearly bare, the top shelf featuring only a box of green tea. Helen would need to venture out soon, make herself presentable and push a cart around a grocery store, pricing vegetables like other women who would go home and employ those same vegetables in the making of nutritious meals for their families. For now, though, the green tea would suffice.

Helen sat at the table, one hand mindlessly engaged in the steeping of the tea while the other rifled through the mail, most of which was still addressed to Scott Plessey. Investing magazines boasting of plans to retire before the age of fifty, put away a million dollars, and finance college savings plans constituted half of her former husband's mail. Scott was a saver and a planner; she had loved that about him, never having to worry about financial matters. He had begun to talk to Robbie about stocks and investing, too early as far as Helen was concerned, teaching his son how a stock could grow in value over time. Scott had stacked multiple Leggo blocks next to a single block in an effort to show how stocks could outgrow and thus tower over the yield a bank account could be expected to deliver.

For Robbie's fifth birthday Scott had purchased one hundred shares of Disney stock, opening an account in the boy's name and insisting that the dividends be mailed directly to Robbie. The checks came quarterly, and Robbie's eyes grew big as he opened the envelopes and withdrew the checks so that he and his daddy could go to the bank together and deposit the check into Robbie's college savings account. Robbie had begun to cross days off the calendar in anticipation of the next dividend check. These 'quarterlies' became like little celebrations, coming every three months and warranting a stop at Baskin Robbins on the way home from the bank.

Helen stacked the magazines and other materials to be recycled. Credit card applications she ripped in half, fearful of identity theft that could ensnare either Scott or herself. The bills Helen put in a small pile under her cup of tea to be dealt with after she had cleared the table of the rest. The last envelope was addressed to Helen Marsh. It had been years since she had seen a piece of mail acknowledging her maiden name. She had been married all of the seven years she and Scott had lived in the house. This letter, postmarked in Portland and bearing no return address, had not been forwarded, the address distinct and written with a steady although light hand. The envelope was oatmeal in color, made from the tiniest articles of pulp that suggested recycling.

Her heart fluttered a bit as she slid her thumb under the flap, slowly opening the wafer-thin envelope. Inside was a single folded piece of paper made from the same paper as the envelope. Helen unfolded it and dropped the paper, *like touching a stove*, the instant she recognized its contents. It was as though the air had been vacuumed out of her lungs, and Helen heard herself suck in a breath after a moment. She felt warmth course through her cheeks as she stared at the paper lying open on the table in front of her. It was a sketch, done in pencil, detailed, accurate, and clearly the hand of a talented artist. With a smile that had always tugged at the strings of her heart, Robbie, as he had looked when Helen had last seen him alive, appeared to be staring at something that both amused and entertained him beyond the artist.

Slowly, as if her hands were directed by another, Helen picked up the sketch of her son, vaguely aware of a numbing sensation crawling over her scalp. Helen reached for the envelope, looked again at both sides and pried it open; *there must be more.* The envelope was empty, and Helen once more turned her attention to the drawing. It resembled a school picture in that it showed the face and collar of the shirt Robbie was wearing, a polka-dotted button-up Helen knew to be hanging in his closet at that very moment.

Conflicting emotions coursed through the woman like an itch that has been scratched too aggressively. Her nerves, still raw, were reminded of the loss, *as if she could ever forget*, but at the same time, looking at the drawing Helen's heart was flooded with an infusion of love for the boy she had birthed. *Who could have sent such a thing?* It was surely meant as a kindness. Why would the sender not allow her to acknowledge the drawing? Helen scanned every inch of the drawing, thinking that maybe some initials were to be found. A magnifying glass from the drawer under the coffee pot allowed her to scrutinize the sketch. Helen thought that maybe she could identify the letter '*M*' in the crease of Robbie's collar but was not any more certain than she'd been when looking for subliminal messaging in a marketing class she had once taken in college.

Whoever had sent the drawing had mailed it from within the same city in which she lived. Which meant that unless it was mailed when passing through, the artist likely lived within miles of Helen. Going through her address book she racked her brain trying to think of who could have sent the drawing. She wasn't certain she even knew anyone with artistic talent. The sketch might have been professional; perhaps someone drew it while looking at a photograph. It was original, not copied or mimeographed, touching an edge lightly with an eraser convinced her of that.

That night Helen poured the first glass of wine she'd had in months, sat on the couch in the living room and stared at the drawing. She couldn't bring herself to perforate the paper with even a pin, instead propping the drawing on top of the fireplace mantle like a greeting card. A strange warmth or comfort came over her, brought on by more than the wine, she suspected.

For several weeks after the sketch arrived, Helen checked her mail eagerly. She found herself tuned in to the sound of the mail van's brakes, which squealed slightly as it stopped in front of her house. There was nothing out of the ordinary in the post, and Helen came to accept that someone, *a distant friend or acquaintance, maybe of Scott's,* had gotten word of Robbie's death and wanted to express their condolences. This thought had caused Helen to check the list of people to whom they had sent Christmas cards, with the notion that maybe the sketch was done by looking at the Plessey's seasonal card. After checking the list and perusing last year's card, Helen concluded that while possible, it didn't seem likely.

The mail van passed Helen as she was turning the corner onto her street after forcing herself to take a walk during an unusually foggy January morning. Helen couldn't see the driver, but waved as the van emitted a short, cheerful honk. It was then that Helen felt an inexplicable hope rise, and while it had been several months since the oatmeal envelope bearing a sketch of her son had arrived, she could not help herself and began to hasten her pace. The mail van stopped briefly, brakes squeaking, at her mailbox and motored on to the next house, its round red brake lights glowing like a demon's eyes in the fog. When the van turned out of sight, Helen allowed herself to break into a jog. By the time she was fifty yards away she found herself in a virtual sprint, her eyes tearing from the cold.

Clutching the small bundle of mail tightly, Helen refrained herself from examining its contents until she was seated at the table. Thumbing through the envelopes *like one desperately scratching a lottery ticket*, Helen's heart leaped when she saw the oatmeal envelope, which was once again postmarked Portland and bore no return address. Careful not to tear the envelope, Helen opened it, her fingers visibly shaking, and withdrew the paper. Robbie's pose was similar to the first sketch, but the drawing was definitely different. Helen scrutinized the artwork as she walked it over to the fireplace and held it above the first picture. Robbie's hair was slightly longer in the second, like it got when Helen would begin to gently prepare him for a trip to the barber. The top Robbie was wearing was an Aqua-man T-shirt, not something Helen would send him to school with on a picture day. The other differences were too subtle to characterize, but Helen was aware of them all the same.

Placing the second picture next to the first, Helen enjoyed a glass of wine that night, curled on the couch, staring blissfully back and forth between the two. None of the first sketch's negative feelings that had commingled with the positive accompanied this second delivery. Helen basked in a bone-deep warmth that inspired the recollection of any number of tender moments she had had with her young son.

The next morning Helen put the second envelope in the large manila envelope in which she had saved the first. Moments later she withdrew them both and held them side-by-side. They were identical save for the date. Helen marked the previous day's date on the calendar with a red *his favorite color* star before going to her part-time job at the public library. All morning, while cataloging books, Helen was plagued by a feeling that she was missing something. It was a nagging feeling connected to the special mail she had received - a dot she was failing to connect.

Upon her return home, Helen took the drawings from the mantle and placed them under a reading light while she scanned every square millimeter with the magnifying glass for the better part of an hour. Nothing. Helen wondered how long it took to create such a drawing. The question was, of course, dwarfed by her curiosity as to whom and why. After leftovers consisting of tuna casserole, Helen pulled the oatmeal envelopes out of the large manila once more. She carefully placed them on the table and went out to the garage and began digging through the recycling bin. Last week she had tossed the previous year's spent calendar in the bin for curbside pickup that was scheduled for the following day. Laying it on the table next to the envelopes, Helen turned the pages until she came to October 18th, the day after the envelope was postmarked in Portland, the day the first oatmeal envelope had been delivered. Her eyes were immediately drawn to the date, as its entire square was filled with Robbie's blunt red crayon that read DIS DIV.

Helen flipped back through the calendar, *wish I could turn back time*, until she came to the previous DIS DIV, this entered in purple crayon. Robbie had filled the entire square on the 18th of July with the letters D I S forcing Scott to write DIV in smaller letters beneath on the 25th. Both sketches of Robbie had arrived on days that Disney paid a quarterly dividend to its shareholders, days that were very important to Robbie. Looking ahead on the current calendar, Helen wrote DIS DIV on the 18th of April and began to anticipate that day's mail with an eagerness that was entirely new to her.

In order to help pass the time Helen began to tear out overgrown shrubbery, weed, and apply new bark dust after planting new bulbs in the front yard. At first she had been reluctant, fearing it would depress her to be working in the soil as she had when Robbie had been a toddler, comforting her with his digging sounds and manly narrative as he played with dump trucks just feet from his mother. Instead, Helen found herself smiling as she recalled some of the playful banter that her uninhibited child had made her privy to. The mail lady commented on how nice the yard would look when the bulbs flowered, and Helen was able to respond with thanks and a smile, both genuine.

As the 18th of April approached Helen tried to prepare herself for what could prove very disappointing. It was, after all, just a theory. What if the dividend dates were merely a coincidence? What if the artist forgot, or had grown weary of this strange game? *Was it a game? No, surely not. But if not, what then?*

The 18th was a rainy day from start to finish. Helen had planned on gardening, looking casual as she took the mail from the carrier. *No sense in putting it in the box since she would be right there.* Instead, Helen sat on the front porch steeping her green tea as the van squeaked to a stop in front of her box. Helen's stomach churned warily as she stood, waiting for the van to pull away. She couldn't wait until getting the bundle inside the house to look, and hunching over to protect the mail from the rain, she thumbed through until she saw the oatmeal envelope.

Thoroughly drying her hands, Helen stared at the envelope on the table. Her stomach rumbled as if a vat of acid had been released within. The seconds before opening the letter reminded her both of Christmas morning and standing on the high dive for the first time as a child. She took a deep breath, exhaled, and opened the envelope.

The third drawing was as different from the second as the second had been from the first. The first thing Helen realized was that the shirt Robbie was wearing was unfamiliar to her. The second thing she noticed was that his hair was cut shorter than she could ever remember it being. The third thing Helen noticed was that her son looked older. Robbie Plessey looked older than he had when he had been taken from her. Helen rushed into the living room and held the sketch up to the right of the first two so that they were all in order. Not only was she certain the third and most recent drawing made Robbie look older, she was now able to see that in the second Robbie looked older than in the first. Helen had heard of computer programs that projected aging in people, both criminals and victims. *Could this be somebody's idea of a sick joke?*

The peace, bliss, and comfort she had been anticipating failed to materialize, and instead Helen found herself deeply troubled as she sat with her glass of red wine in front of the fireplace that evening. It couldn't have been the alcohol because Helen put down the glass after only a sip as she found herself deluged with dark thoughts. *What if Robbie wasn't really dead? What if he were alive somewhere? What if he had been kidnapped and was being raised by another family? What if he was scared, cold, hungry, and calling for her at that very moment?*

This was foolish she told herself. Helen had seen her son's body. Not to identify him; Scott had done that, but to say goodbye. Scott had warned her not to do it, but Helen had insisted, sensing somehow that she needed the closure, even before framing the notion in such a context. Scott had stood slightly behind her as if prepared to catch her in the event she fainted. But Helen had not fainted. Instead, she brushed back a lock of Robbie's hair and kissed a small scar at the peak of his forehead where he had run into the island in the kitchen. There could be no doubt, Robbie, her son who would never find love, was dead, and Helen purged the residual *what ifs* from her mind.

Nonetheless, she got up, took the third sketch from the fireplace, and walked upstairs to Robbie's room. At the only grief counseling session Helen and Scott had attended, the counselor spoke of the tendency to keep a deceased child's room like a shrine or mausoleum. There were differing schools of thought, but it was generally believed that families should be encouraged to wait until they were ready to deal with the room rather than purge it right away. Scott didn't care, saying he couldn't make himself go into the room regardless of its decor. Helen had cried herself to sleep in the room for several nights following the accident, sprawled face down on Robbie's Spiderman comforter, inhaling deeply through her nose in an effort to keep the memory of what Robbie smelled like fresh in her mind. Since the first sketch had arrived, Helen had only gone in to the room to dust, once opening a window to allow for several hours of fresh air.

The door opened with a squeak that reminded Helen of the brakes on the mail van. It had squeaked when they bought the house, and Helen had stopped Scott from oiling the door once, insisting that she wanted to hear if Robbie opened the door at night. They had both laughed, probably imagining their son sneaking out as a teen. Helen flicked on the light switch and went to Robbie's closet. The polka-dotted shirt was hanging with the rest of his button-downs, and the Aqua-man shirt was neatly folded in a drawer. There was, however, no shirt even resembling the one worn in the drawing that had come in the mail not six hours earlier.

Downstairs again, Helen scrutinized the third drawing with the magnifying glass once more, particularly the shirt that was of a pattern featuring gentle whorls of varying sizes. She wished the color could be determined, but the lead pencil provided no clues in that direction, only shades. Robbie looked healthy and happy, of that there could be no denying. He would have been six in three weeks, and Helen found herself hoping that another drawing would come on that day. *A bonus, like extra credit or icing on the cake.*

When sleep finally came to Helen late that night it was the third picture she saw, the colors of Robbie's shirt changing, the whorls spinning, becoming closer, then farther away like an optical illusion. Helen awoke with a gasp and sat up in bed. *If Robbie was as he looked, that is to say older, then he was likely larger. After all, he was a growing boy! And if he had grown it was possible that his old shirts no longer fit him.* Helen raced downstairs and held the second sketch under a reading lamp. Try as she might though, Helen could not discern if the Aqua-man shirt was tight on her son.

Robbie's birthday came but unaccompanied by a fourth sketch. Disappointed, Helen reset her sights on the 18th of July when Disney issued their next dividend. At the end of June an annual report issued by the company came in the mail. An augmented magazine of sorts, it was addressed to a Mr. Robert Plessey. It was an impressive colored brochure, the paper thick and expensive feeling. The report prominently featured glossy pictures of happy employees and multitudes of pleased patrons mingling with a wide host of magical Disney characters in parks that were now scattered in numerous countries about the globe. Helen thumbed absentmindedly through the brochure remembering fondly the only time they had taken Robbie. She had worried initially that he might be afraid of the larger than life Disney figures, but the young shareholder had approached Goofy, Mickey, and Donald with a child's innocence, enthusiasm, and wonder.

As she flipped the brochure onto the coffee table Helen noticed a small claim to use recycled paper on the back cover. It made her think of the envelopes the sketches had come inside. *Maybe the brochure held some special message.* It was a stretch, but something she could not afford to dismiss, and for the next several hours Helen scanned every word, number, chart, and graph in the report. Finally, she tossed it back on the coffee table and shrugged her shoulders in resignation before glancing up at the three sketches lined up in the order she had received them.

The fourth sketch left no doubt in Helen's mind that Robbie was getting older, bigger. *Growing up before my very eyes, except in quarterly installments,* she thought sardonically. And then, arranging the drawings so they were evenly spaced across the mantle, Helen caught herself. *Robbie's dead. I lost my son. People who lose loved ones never see or hear from them again. And yet, here I am, repeatedly receiving a gift on a regular basis that I anticipate with joy. A gift that makes me happy, gives me comfort. I may never hold Robbie again, but these quarterly sketches are a blessing nonetheless. I must be grateful.* Helen could hear her own mother telling her many times throughout her childhood that life is what we make of it. *Could it be,* Helen wondered, *that death too, is what we make of it?*

This adjustment in her outlook marked a turning point for Helen and was, no doubt, at least partially responsible for her thumbing through rather than recycling the fall community college class schedule that came in the mail a week later. The idea of going back to school intrigued her, and many of the art, writing, and literature classes looked fun and interesting.

Helen had been prepared to be the oldest student in her classes and was pleasantly surprised to find she was closer to the median, many of her classmates starting second careers. At first she merely listened to discussions, choosing to hear her peers' opinions and takes on readings. Weighing her own thoughts against those voiced by others soon convinced Helen that she was worthy of being heard as well. Getting a high mark on a creative writing assignment gave Helen more of a thrill than she could ever remember as an undergraduate or even high school student. The stimulation and purpose the classes provided soon had Helen considering getting her teaching license and pursuing a career path she had abandoned shortly after meeting Scott.

Sketch number five featured a slight freckling on Robbie's face and a mesh jersey of sorts, maybe soccer or baseball? Instead of bangs, his hair was now swept neatly to a side, and Helen saw her own eyes in his for the first time, something that Scott had seen from the start. Something else occurred to her for the first time; *could Scott be getting sketches of their son as well? Would he tell her if he was?* Helen reasoned that she had not told her former husband or really even considered it. She did not know his address or even if he was still living in Oregon. She supposed she could contact his parents, but they had not reached out to her since their son had left Helen.

That night, Helen developed a theory that she would hold onto for a good many years - a dual theory actually. Her mind's attempt to rationalize the strange phenomenon to which she regarded herself a grateful recipient, had deduced that either Robbie, and therefore likely others, continued to live out their disrupted temporal lives in heaven or perhaps Helen was simply being shown glimpses of what would have been. And while she knew that others would laugh at these notions, preferring to believe that a mysterious stranger was responsible, Helen had gradually begun to dismiss the idea of a stranger, for it seemed antithetical to her understanding of human nature for a person to do this without revealing more and more of themselves or their game over time.

The few times Helen had had someone over to the house since receiving the first drawing she had taken the pictures from the mantle and placed them carefully on Robbie's bed before closing the door. She had not known how to explain the drawings and wasn't even certain she wanted to try. Even when her sister had visited, Helen hadn't wanted to share, uncertain as to whether it was just too private or out of fear that revealing the quarterlies to another might make them stop, *like breaking a spell.*

Helen was briefly startled when she opened the sixth envelope; a bottom tooth was missing from her son's mischievous smile. The seventh and eighth sketches featured several gaps each in the boy's smile, and bigger permanent teeth filling previous holes. After perching the ninth drawing, Helen realized her modest mantle could not take a tenth, and she went to the craft store and bought several dozen identical picture frames from a puzzled cashier. Before framing the sketches, Helen carefully made copies on her printer at home. As with small books that can make a drawing appear to move like frames in an eight-millimeter film, Helen flipped through her bound copies, smiling as she achieved a similar effect. Helen considered hanging the framed pictures in Robbie's room but quickly realized she wouldn't enjoy them as much. She had found that she admired the pictures while she ate, paid bills, read, wrote her papers, and even watched an occasional television program. Helen was not embarrassed to admit to herself that the pictures provided her with a level of solace and even companionship, despite realizing how sad that might seem to others.

Less than a year later, Helen began her student teaching practicum in a fourth grade classroom at an elementary school less than five miles from her home. The assignment placed her with students a year or two older than Robbie would be, and at first Helen was leery. However, it was at this school Helen learned not only that she enjoyed being around the children, but also that she might yet entertain the idea of romance, an idea that had long been dormant.

Mark Kasik had a firm command of the group of nine and ten year olds in his class and a sense of security that allowed him to gradually and adeptly help transition Helen into the role of primary teacher. He willingly spent hours with Helen, offering praise and advice not only on how to teach, but how to deal with parents and approach upcoming interviews. Nearing fifty, Mark had a great deal of experience and was open and sharing with his knowledge.

The following year Helen was hired by the same district in which she had student taught and was assigned a third grade class at a school not much farther from her house. She continued seeing Mark; going over to his house for dinners he seemed to enjoy cooking for her. Her former mentor teacher was divorced with two grown sons, both living in Washington. He had long been accustomed to living on his own, but clearly wanted Helen to be a part of his life. Several times they went out to dinner, and on one occasion Mark asked when he was going to get to see her place. Helen swirled the wine in her glass and studied her companion. She had told him about losing her son one evening the previous year while waiting for parents who were late to a student conference. The parents showed up, and the subject was dropped. Helen knew there were questions Mark had wanted to ask and was endeared that he didn't bring the subject up, instead waiting for her to broach the topic in her own good time.

"You remember I told you I lost my son, Robbie," Helen replied carefully. "That was only part of the story."

Helen studied Mark's face as she flipped on the lights to her living room. The man said nothing, merely studying the pictures, taking them in one by one. After a moment, Helen went into the kitchen and came back with two glasses of wine, one of which she handed to Mark. He took the glass and put his other arm around her. Together they studied the chronology of pictures, Helen trying to see it for the first time through Mark's eyes.

"Any thoughts?" Helen finally prompted.

"Report cards," Mark said simply, unable to take his eyes from the wall.

"Excuse me?"

"They're report cards of sorts. A visual report card or update."

Helen smiled, taking in the idea. "I call them my *quarterlies*. But *report card* works."

"Miraculous. Simply miraculous," Mark beamed.

"Am I to take it you don't think some crazy relative is sending them?"

"More likely an angel," Mark said without mirth. "You are truly blessed, Helen."

It was this reaction that allowed Helen to open the floodgates to her heart once more. Helen had been prepared for the normally pragmatic teacher to insist upon a practical solution to the enigma, for him to break it down and deduce a conclusion based on fact, logic, reason, and rationale, like the stripping away of oil paint layer by layer until only ugly, raw canvass remained. But the opposite had occurred. Within mere minutes Mark had not only allowed but declared the phenomenon to be a blessing, and so it remained.

The following summer Mark and Helen were married in a small outdoor ceremony attended by both of Mark's sons, Helen's sister, and several of Mark's former students, now grown. It impressed Helen that his students had thought enough of Mark to stay in contact with the man through the years. If for only the mail, the couple chose to make Helen's house their home.

Opening the seventeenth envelope Helen realized that somewhere along the line Robbie had become supplemental in her life rather than the focus. And while the phrase seemed trite, Helen knew that she *had* been given a second chance at happiness. In between the classroom and her husband, Helen was leading a full and rich life once again. The quarterlies, or report cards as Mark called them, allowed Robbie to stay close in her heart and mind, growing well beyond the colorless boy who had lain cold and still on a stainless steel table top at the morgue. The drawings replaced that image, allowing an invisible appendage to taper off rather than being chopped off, nerves left raw and exposed. Closure, it was said, is good, but Helen enjoyed the window to Robbie's life being left open a crack, allowing for a gust of fresh air every three months.

Somewhere in the early forties, the sketches still

numbered in her mind, Helen began to detect peach fuzz on Robbie's neck and chin. No longer was he her little boy. He was becoming a handsome young man, his smile broad and freckles deepening. The fifty-first through fifty-fourth sketches featured Robbie with longer side burns and a goatee like those worn by so many young men of the day. Helen thought he looked a bit ridiculous and giggled in spite of herself. *Probably experimenting*, she reasoned, *it's only natural.*

Then one day shortly after Helen had retired, she and Mark were opening the seventy-ninth oatmeal envelope and were shocked to find the sketch revealed a startling change. The nearly two decades long consistent size of Robbie within the sketch had been greatly reduced! Now Robbie was featured alongside, *quite close,* to a beautiful young lady who was smiling as proudly as Robbie himself.

Helen's eyes were wide, and her throat suddenly felt dry. She put a hand to her gaping mouth and stared in shock at the drawing. *What could it mean?* Mark laughed out loud and declared with a joyous roar, "Robbie's gotten married! Your boy's taken a bride, Helen!" Tears of joy flooded from Helen's eyes at the thought, and she was instantly convinced that Mark was right. Robbie *had* found love.

That night, long after Mark had begun to snore gently, Helen got up and went downstairs for another peek at the picture of Robbie and his bride. Helen wished she knew the young woman's name. *Had she been someone who had also died? Could she still be alive and simply be the woman Robbie would have married if he had lived? If so, could it be that she had married, or would marry another man since Robbie Plessey would not be coming her way? Either way, could her family be close, live in the area? Would she have been someone Robbie would have met in college?* Regardless of the possible answers to these questions and many more Helen felt a warmth toward the girl who would be her daughter-in-law and drifted off to sleep on the couch while gently embracing the image of the young couple.

The next morning over coffee and tea, Helen told Mark that she wanted to see if they could learn who the woman was, and Mark had looked over his newspaper and responded, "If you can tell me one possible good that could come of learning her identity, I'll help you."

Stunned, Helen sat holding her bag of tea above the lip of the cup as it dawned on her that it might *not* be good to know, that no good *could* come of any discovery.

Mark had returned to reading the paper. "You might as well just give her a name that you like, and wait until one of these portraits has a *third* party." Helen gulped, dropping the bag of tea into the cup.

Mark had been half right. Exactly two years later, a sketch showed up in the mail prominently featuring Robbie and *Amy,* as she had become, holding twins. It took Helen another year to become convinced they were girls, as they finally had enough hair to sport ribbons.

Years later, when Mark Kasik died peacefully in his sleep at the age of seventy-five, Robbie's depiction was that of a nearly middle-aged man, his hair taking on a different shading, the underneath of his jaw hanging slightly lower, the tiniest lines at the corners of his eyes now visible. Helen realized that her husband had almost certainly been right when he referred to the report cards as being both a blessing and miraculous. Had they been drawn by someone Scott and Helen had known long ago the artist would likely be quite old by now.

Helen busied herself with gardening when the Oregon weather would allow and reading and writing short stories when it would not. It was in this fashion that Mrs. Helen Kasik enjoyed her golden years, the quarterly updates coming in the form of sketches which saw her *grandchildren* growing up healthy and beautiful, the pride evident in their parents' faces.

When Helen's time approached she was not surprised, her heart having fluttered strangely throughout a cold she had been fighting. She was lying on the couch in front of her gas fireplace, looking at the array of pictures that nearly filled two walls now. They resembled a guided tour down memory lane for the blind; that is to say she needed to fill in so many blanks for herself, utilizing the sparse clues provided by the sketches and their subjects.

As Helen began to slip into a deep sleep from which she would not waken, her mind took her back to her childhood. She was in a tree fort in her friend Olivia's back yard. Helen and Olivia were dangling their feet over the edge of the fort's decking, dropping daisy pedals as they were pulled one by one. It was a lazy summer day, and the girls were talking about boys, school, books, and anything else they could think of to pass the time.

Helen asked Olivia if she believed in God. "I don't know. Do you?" Olivia responded.

"I don't know. Sometimes, maybe," Helen returned.

"Do you believe in heaven?"

"I don't know. I guess so. I mean I'd like to think there's a heaven after life on earth," Helen said honestly. Both girls were quiet for a moment before Helen asked, "Olivia, are you scared of dying?"

"Sure. Isn't everyone?" Olivia responded.

"I suppose so. I know I am."

"Let's make a deal," Olivia proposed.

"What kind of deal?"

"Whoever dies first has to come back and tell the one still living if everything's okay after you die," Olivia said excitedly.

"What if we can't? I mean, what if we we're not allowed to?"

"I don't know. But if it was me I know I'd think of something," Olivia mused.

"Okay. It's a deal," Helen said.

"Okay, then. Let's swear on it."

Helen crossed her heart with her index finger. "Cross my heart. Now you."

Olivia, who had moved to the coast less than a year later, crossed her heart as well. "Cross my heart."

Mr. P

In preparing for the first week of my final year teaching school, I've become quite nostalgic. This year will be the thirtieth year repeating a cycle I have come to know quite well. The students will come in to middle school wide-eyed and a bit intimidated, having heard horror stories from older siblings, friends, and such. They will be subjected to short clipped speeches dealing with rules and procedures from teachers, many of who are just as nervous. None of the information in these speeches is retained or even heard for that matter. By the second day, a character or two will have emerged from the ranks, students eager to achieve a bit of notoriety among their peers. Quite often these are students who are neglected at home and have been bored to the point where they actually look forward to the resumption of school in the fall. Negative attention from an adult is preferred to no attention, as it turns out.

As Halloween approaches the weather turns, and students find they have grown used to getting up early. Routines are established, friendships cemented, and the year begins to pick up steam, marching through the calendar with purpose. Soon the holidays beckon, and hope flickers among students and staff alike that a snowstorm could deposit just enough snow to warrant the suspension of all academic enterprise.

Christmas Vacation looms large, both good and bad depending on one's home life. For teachers, it is almost always a welcome respite, an island to cling to in the seemingly endless sea that is a full school year. Many students look forward to it, having built

Christmas into a nearly magical event. The expectation is nearly always greater than the day itself and fades with mild disappointment, unable to live up to past Christmases, when youthful innocence was still fully intact. For a few, the two-week vacation approaches with a sense of pending doom. Realities involving unemployment, drugs, alcohol, and tattered marriages serve to mar the fortnight.

The first week in January is marked by a dull apathy. Sunlight is scarce, and teenagers who have grown accustomed to sleeping in have trouble acclimating themselves to the routine they had carved but months earlier. Rooms are stuffy and quite often too hot or cold due to antiquated, loud, and temperamental radiators connected to boiler rooms kept working thanks to duct tape and innovative custodians. Teachers readjust their sights to spring break and begin to tackle projects, scoring assignments, and state tests that must be administered before the weather turns. A sense of drudgery sets in as the novelty of the New Year has long since worn away, and the coming summer seems too distant to contemplate.

Spring break is almost cruel in its unwillingness to linger. It seems to end before it has begun, reminding one of Tantalus, whose eternal thirst was frustrated by cool water up to his chin. Having sampled freedom, both students and staff are reminded they must buckle under for the long haul. Summer is still several months away, and there is much that must be done before it arrives. As the rainy season fades, hot weather emerges in an intermittent fashion. June has students staring out windows thinking of ice cream, sprinklers, air conditioning, community pools, and lounging on a couch or front stoop, no longer burdened by expectations of homework or early rising. The more introspective among the student body begin to realize how much they've changed during the course of the year and how long ago Halloween seems.

The middle of June brings end of the year activities, student body election speeches, band and orchestra performances, dances, county track meets, final exams, and an assembly or two. Finally, yearbooks are dispensed and signed, tears are shed, good-byes are said, and the halls, in desperate need of waxing, grow quiet and still at last.

Despite a thousand books I want to read, projects I plan to do, and trips I hope to take, I promise myself I will enjoy this last year before retirement. None of the books, projects, or trips will be like the first few months of school, where getting to know the students and their talents is like diving for oysters, acutely aware that each shell has the possibility of housing a magnificent pearl. I think back on all the students I've known over the course of twenty-nine years, and while I'd be hard pressed to remember all their names, I can honestly say each has left an indelible mark on me. I hope and believe that many, dare say I most, are truly fine citizens, and I entertain the thought that just maybe, I am, in a tiny way, responsible for a sliver of their development.

A great deal of this nostalgic flood is due to the coming of my final year, no doubt, but to say that this is the only reason would be untrue. For just last week, I had a chance encounter that reminded me of why I got into the profession in the first place.

To my fellow fifth graders, Mr. Pete Panetti walked on water. I can still remember the joy I felt when, after tearing open the letter that bore the return address of Mable Rush Elementary, I learned that Mr. Panetti was to be my fifth grade teacher. There were three classes in each grade, and I hadn't liked my chances. Everyone wanted to be in Mr. P's class, and I knew a lot of parents requested him, mothers in particular, who referred to the man as Peter Pan when talking among themselves. It was a source of contention with my mother, who didn't believe in asking for favors. She insisted we would let the chips fall where they may, for I had to get used to all kinds of teachers and not always get what I wanted.

As fourth graders, we had watched Mr. P play football with the fifth graders. At six and a half feet in height, he looked as Gulliver might have as he danced among his many charges. Each play would take about fifteen seconds as he insisted the ball be returned to the new line of scrimmage and hiked in short order, so as to milk as many plays out of a recess period as possible. He distributed the ball softly and with perfectly deft placement to all the kids equally, boys and girls, fast and slow, thick and thin alike. They didn't always catch it but received a word or two of encouragement from the hurler that had them believing they would reel in the next one.

The conclusion of each recess where football was played amazes me to this day. Mr. P would launch a football some sixty yards in the air toward the laundry cart that held all the sporting equipment. Then, one of us would toss him the other ball, which we brought out in case we lost the first over the schoolyard fence. With his other hand, Mr. P would throw the second ball which traced an identical arc through the air and landed in the cart, just as the first had. I saw several balls bounce out, but during my entire fifth grade year, I never saw Mr. P miss the equipment cart with either his left or right hand.

Able to *dribble* a football as easily as we could bounce a basketball, Mr. P made other games fun as well. He never shot and always passed when playing hoops. Foursquare and wall ball were made more interesting because of the constant and good-natured banter with which he engaged us all. When it came to dodgeball, we all laughed because Mr. P threw the ball with a two-hand chest pass and not all that hard. When asked why he threw that way, he said he didn't want to hurt anyone. We laughed until he used a ball to dislodge another that was wedged in the fork of a tree branch one day. The ball he threw actually whistled and hummed as it moved like a laser toward the intended target, which popped free like a cork upon impact.

As a kid, I lived for recess with Mr. P, but as a teacher, I can now see that his true genius shone in the classroom. While never playing favorites, the man had the ability to make each of us feel as though we were in some way special, not only to him, but the world at large. Claiming that everyone had an undiscovered vein of genius or talent, he made certain you left his class convinced you'd found yours. His contention that I was blessed with a 'soft spoken eloquence' inspired my love of writing that lasts to this day.

Mr. P was so much fun that you were never aware of the time in his class, even as recess or the end of the day approached. Part of the reason was that he left the clock unplugged, and it read 9:37 for every minute of the fifth grade. In the midst of a session where we were working on an assignment or project, Mr. P would announce, "Ten more minutes until we switch gears."

Once, Jimmy Forrester, noting that Mr. P never wore a watch, asked him how he would know when the ten minutes were up. Mr. P looked at his bare wrist and said simply, "Jimmy, it's 10:14 now. At 10:24 we'll move on to math." Jimmy looked at the new digital watch he'd been sporting since his birthday the previous week. He looked at me, shrugged, and nodded his head, acknowledging that it was, in fact, 10:14. Jimmy showed me his wrist when Mr. P told us to take out our math books. 10:24, on the dot. Unfailingly, at 2:58, Mr. P would have us pack up for home, the bell ringing exactly two minutes later.

There was no shortage to Mr. P's strange and wondrous talents and abilities. Students have long wondered about teachers able to hear things thought to be out of range. Mr. P did that ability one better. On more than one occasion he darted a knowing look my way, as I was about to say something to a friend I wouldn't want my mother to hear. From time to time, expressions on the faces of my friends suggested I was not alone in being deterred by such a pedagogic and pre-emptive look.

This, however, paled when compared with Mr. P's ability to tell whether one was lying. The Monday following Halloween we all brought in our remaining bounty from the festive evening. After the morning recess, Sharon Hill reported her bag of candy missing. Mr. P lined us all up, backs against the chalkboard and sat at one of the desks in the front row with his hand on his chin. He squinted as his eyes roved back and forth, pausing for a fraction of a second on each student. After two or three minutes of scrutiny Mr. P frowned and suddenly dismissed us to our music class. The next morning

Aaron Fipp's mother was seen leaving school as the busses pulled up. Aaron, who had to stay after school three days scraping gum from under the bleachers, told us that Mr. P had simply whispered to him on the way back from music, advising him to return Sharon's candy during lunch when all the kids were eating or at recess.

While I hated to see lunch recess end, it led to my favorite part of the day in the classroom. Upon our return, we were to get a drink of water and sit down at our desks where we were to rest our heads, cradled in our folded arms. Mr. P would turn off the lights, and as our heart rates began to slow, he would read aloud from a classic of his choosing. His deep, rich voice brought to life <u>Tom Sawyer</u>, <u>Treasure Island</u>, <u>Gulliver's Travels</u>, <u>The Black Stallion</u>, and so many more characters and stories. I would close my eyes and become immersed in the world he created by reading with bold expression and voices that were not his own. Like waking from a dream you wanted to never end, it seemed like just minutes later that our collective reverie was broken by the return of Mr. P's regular voice, "Heads or tails?" he would unfailingly call. After the first few weeks of school this was greeted with a chorus of groans because it soon became evident that Mr. P never lost the coin toss that determined whether he was to keep reading for an additional ten minutes. It didn't matter whose coin it was, and he always let one of us make the call. He NEVER lost a coin toss. We had heard of this phenomenon from older kids, but hadn't believed it until we'd seen it for ourselves – month after month.

As a matter of fact, Mr. P seemed to have a strange power over coins. He could bend a penny with his bare hands, straining and contorting his face for effect as the penny began to yield to fingers so long they could swallow a baseball, middle finger touching thumb like a flesh seam. When asked if he could bend a quarter, Mr. P frowned and asked why anyone would want to waste such a sum. Able to balance forty quarters on his elbow, Mr. P deftly dropped the joint and without fail was able to open his palm and reveal all forty coins, still uniformly stacked. I was spraying small stacks of quarters all over my mother's kitchen for a week after I first saw that bit of legerdemain. That our teacher was able to produce coins from behind our ears at any given moment hardly came as a surprise as we came to know him.

Life in Mr. P's class was more than fun and games though. He got results. I only came to realize how much I'd learned and grown academically the next year as I found myself ahead of my peers in most of my classes for the first time. I saw kids relying on calculators for times tables, and I would smile, remembering my cut-out jersey being the third to be retired and hung on the wall in Mr. P's class after demonstrating mastery of my multiplication tables. In addition, I continued reading books by the same authors as Mr. P had read to us.

U.S. History was my favorite subject, as Mr. P conveyed his historical understanding by drawing us into the dates and events we studied. He would close his eyes and interpret history as might be seen through the eyes of a youngster who had lived it, immersing us in details not seen in our texts. His portrayal of events made them seem truly relevant as he demonstrated how they impacted lives really lived by people in times somehow connected to our own.

Dealing with behavioral issues has always been a problem for some teachers. Aside from the missing candy I can only remember one other incident where Mr. P had to exert himself in this regard. We were doing an exercise on locating information in anticipation of needing such skills for the upcoming state test. Working in pairs, we shared a book of Yellow Pages. Mr. P would announce a service we might find ourselves needing to call on someday. We were to find the name, address, and phone number of the business that might best service this need. Carl Gentry and Steve Payton were wrestling over the phone book, each wanting to take charge, when they realized Mr. P was looming behind them. He picked up the telephone book, and you could have heard an ant breathe when he began to slowly rip it in two equal halves. Mr. P placed a half on each boy's desk and merely smiled as he proclaimed in a quiet but amiable voice, "Problem solved."

That was as menacing as it got. I think we all viewed Mr. P's classroom as a sanctuary, where nothing could hurt us, the rich and familiar smell of his coffee putting us all at ease. During school hours, it was as though we were enveloped in a protective womb where bad or evil influences were kept at bay. Whether it was listening to him read or the times when he brought in his acoustic guitar and sang old cowboy ballads, mixing and weaving our names in with the melodies, we always felt safe and valued in Mr. P's presence.

It was after Christmas vacation that we came to realize Mr. P's protective umbrella did not extend beyond the school grounds. The day before the winter break began we were listening to Christmas carols on an old tape player while stringing popcorn that escaped our mouths, and gluing loops of green and red construction paper into a chain that seemingly had no beginning. Mr. P was circulating around the room visiting with the various groups of students who were splayed out on tables, desks, and the floor. He always circulated during group work, making his way from group to group. *Taking our pulse*, he called it.

After making his rounds, Mr. P poured himself a cup of coffee and settled into a desk where Eddie Gonzalez and Gary Tish were working on a chain that kept coming unglued. Mr. P looked like a praying mantis contorted into a fifth grader's desk. I couldn't hear what he was saying, but I could see Eddie nod from time to time. Soon Mr. P asked Gary if he would take something to the office, and Gary proudly marched out the door with an envelope I now suspect was empty. Mr. P continued talking to Eddie, both looking somber as though the subject matter was of much gravity. Eddie stopped working on the chain and looked at Mr. P. Both nodded at the same time as though they had reached an understanding. Mr. P looked weary and stiff as he got out of the desk and gave our class the two-minute warning.

As soon as I opened the passenger side door to our oversized station wagon, my mother asked if I had remembered a library book that was long overdue from our public library. I trudged back into the building and headed for my classroom, hoping Mr. P hadn't locked the door. The door was still open, and I walked in to find Mr. P at his desk. His hands were clasped as if in prayer, his eyes were closed, and for the first time he looked very old. Not sure if he was actually praying or just had a headache, I stood still, feeling like a stranger encroaching on his alone time. The man who always appeared light-hearted and cheerful was now clearly burdened. It was like seeing Oz after Toto pulled back the curtain. Not that there was anything fraudulent about Mr. P, but that there was more to him than could be seen between the bells marking the start and conclusion of each school day. He smiled weakly and wished me a safe and wonderful vacation after I had retrieved the library book from my desk. I bid him goodbye and joined the exodus of teachers eager to begin their holiday.

Before the resumption of school, I heard about Eddie Gonzalez's parents from my mother who was talking to Jimmy Forrester's mother on the phone. Eddie's father had shot his mother in a drunken rage before turning the gun on himself. Eddie and his sister were at their grandparents' house and now stood to extend that visit into the foreseeable future. I leaned against and slid down the wall in the adjacent mudroom where I had been putting on gloves and galoshes. All I could think about was Eddie and Mr. P talking in such a somber way. Could Mr. P have sensed what the winds held for Eddie's family? Was that why he looked so sad and troubled when I returned for the book?

During my career I've had tragedy befall any number of students' families. I can only hope I've handled such situations with even a fraction of the cathartic skill Mr. P exercised when we returned to school early that January. With our desks rounded in a circle, we listened as Mr. P explained the facts, as published by the local paper, and diffused any rumors and speculation that arose. Our first writing assignment of the New Year involved a letter of support to Eddie Gonzalez. Mr. P assured us he would see to it that Eddie received our missives, and no one doubted his word.

On the last day of school our class voted to have lunch in our own room. We rounded the wagons and ate at our desks. Behind the excitement and nervousness of summer being just hours away and a new school awaiting us in the fall, we were all aware that the end of something special was at hand. As lunch was winding down, Mr. P went to his coat closet and pulled out a big paper grocery bag. He stood behind his desk, opened the sack and pulled out a strange looking, hollow cookie. Staring at the cookie, Mr. P would call us up by name and bestow the efforts of his home cooking upon us one at a time. All the cookies looked pretty much the same to me, but inside these poor imitations of what appeared to be fortune cookies, was a different message for each student handwritten on a yellow slip of paper. The room buzzed as we all compared *fortunes* until the recess bell sounded.

I suspect I knew from the start of fifth grade that I wanted to be a teacher when I grew up. Occasionally, if I didn't have practice or in between seasons, I would drop by my old school and visit Mr. P. I had planned to ask him if I could observe and maybe even help out a bit as part of my high school career orientation project. It was not to be, though, as I learned late in my junior year that Mr. P no longer taught in our district. He had evidently moved away, and no one at my former elementary school was able to offer any kind of forwarding address.

Through the years, I've often thought of Mr. P; my wonderment mixed with curiosity and gratitude. This past week, I've thought of him far more than ever before. I spent much of it driving through the Carolinas enjoying my last week of vacation. Evidently they start school a week earlier than do we. I passed an elementary school and watched as the kids, nearly all black, poured from the building onto the deadened grass of their playing field. Trailing them was a very tall, white, lanky figure *dribbling* a football. I pulled to the side of the road and retrieved my field glasses from the leather satchel I always take birding. I sat in a cold sweat my air conditioner could not quell as I concluded that Mr. P *had not aged a day in nearly a half century.*

The students marched back into the school, following the deposit of both footballs in a wire cart from some sixty yards. I sat in the car, my open wallet on the passenger seat. In my hand was a faded and worn yellow slip of paper that read,

Mark, Your soft-spoken eloquence and writing talent will allow you to influence a great many.

P.P.

A Better Place

Dec. 19, 2005

Dear Mark,

In going through Mom's things I found some of Dad's old stuff as well. And while it may all be water under the bridge, I feel this notebook goes a long way in explaining why Dad was the way he was, at least the last decade or so of his life.

I know it's been years since we've spoken, and I don't figure this will change that, but he was your father just as much as he was mine, and I figure you're entitled to see for yourself.

Best wishes,
Tom

April 12, 1999

Tom and Mark,

As I know the end is near, I feel compelled to explain myself in hopes of not only allowing you to see why I seemed so obsessed these past eleven years, but to possibly shed some light that will allow you both to find God for yourselves. I know religion is a highly personal matter, and we've not always seen eye to eye on the subject. I judge neither of you, as judgment is not mine to make.

Tom, I know your politics make religion the fodder of the simpleminded and superstitious. You likened my finding religion so late in life to those who wrote big checks to the church in hopes of buying their way into heaven. Perhaps, in my case, this is to some extent true. I can only say that my faith is genuine, and I accept God's judgement either way.

Mark, I know the senseless loss of a child has blinded you with a rage that has rendered you unable to appreciate the mystery of God's ways. I can hardly pretend I wouldn't feel the same way, were I in your shoes. I only know with certainty that Bethany is in a better place. I pray that you achieve the peace of mind in someday knowing this.

As you both know, I was a corrections officer at Sing Sing when we lived in Ossining while you were growing up. What you don't know is the following.

The crime rate nationwide and in New York in particular had skyrocketed in the late sixties, and politicians were making big promises about bringing it down. Determined to look tough on crime, they jockeyed with one another in an attempt to fire up Big Surge and clean out Death Row. They were sure that it would serve as a deterrent to anyone contemplating a capital crime. Texans, it seemed, never allowed their chairs to cool down, and the politicians in Albany pointed to lower Lone Star crime rates as justification.

The winds of change being what they were, I soon found myself transferred from the relative calm of D Block to *The Row* as it was called, by inmates and prison personnel alike. D Block housed fellows that could see some light at the end of the tunnel. They understood how to pare down a sentence with good behavior and an earnest demeanor at parole hearings. There was, for most, a good deal of incentive to keep their nose clean. They measured time in days, weeks, months, and years, not altogether unlike a man awaiting his next vacation, or even retirement.

The Row was different. There was no light at

the end of the tunnel. It was more like a black hole that ended with a black sack over your head. Incentive didn't exist. With nothing to lose and nothing to gain, the inmates were often inclined to take you down if the opportunity existed. It was common for inmates to hurl any and all matter of human bodily fluid at guards or each other, for reasons ranging from boredom to avenging slights, both real and imagined.

Most guards stored several change of clothes in their lockers. Some still went home smelling of sewage. Of course, the guards were not without recourse. Often times several guards who had experienced similar humiliations of late would end a shift by having a blanket party, where they would enter a cell and beat on an inmate who was asleep under his blanket.

Some guards got it worse than others, with a correlation existing between the guards that exhibited a measure of cruelty and those that didn't. They took it pretty easy on me. I guess they figured I was fair, not out to make their miserable existence any worse, and just wanted to go home to my family at the end of each shift. Anyway, I got along okay with most of the guys doing the *Final Stretch*, or just *The Stretch* to most.

Don't get me wrong. I wasn't pals with these guys. The vast majority of them were stone cold killers who would brag about and even embellish their murderous deeds. They'd kill you if it'd put ten dollars in their pocket, even if they didn't have a place to spend it. Some were unlikely killers, the sort who killed their wives after walking in on them with another man, killers who made it hard to imagine a repeat performance, but who had nonetheless taken a life and were waiting to give one back. A few would protest their innocence to anyone who'd listen. Most of them had killed again on the inside and found it harder to make a compelling case in a place with all too few sympathetic ears.

Toward the end of my third year on the Row I met an inmate who was unlike any other I had encountered. Jimmy Bitz was a middle-aged black man who had been sentenced to death for the killing of a teacher at the school where he served as night custodian. Jimmy had been a custodian at the school for twenty-three years and had a paper-thin file, as he garnered no complaints or praise, just working in the obscure silence that night at a school affords. Students and staff would come in day after day to clean floors and give precious little thought as to how they got that way.

Jimmy's tenure at the school ended the same day as Mary Ellen Hayes', when the day custodian found Jimmy kneeling over her body with a bloody baseball bat from the P.E. department in his hands. No motive was ever established, and it's unlikely that the authorities really believed Jimmy did it since they spent several weeks pursuing other means. But coming up with nothing, the district attorney's office succumbed to public pressure to close the case. At least that's the way Jimmy told it.

Jimmy's nature was gentle, and he was so soft spoken you had to get close to hear him when he spoke. At first I was leery that he wanted to draw me in close, but Jimmy was the sort to shoo a fly away rather than swat at it. He didn't swear, brag or engage in much talk through the bars with the other prisoners.

The man just sat in his cell reading day after day. A lot of the fellows read (this was before the days of televisions in every cell), but mostly it was just magazines and maybe a trashy novel or two with lascivious passages well dog-eared. Jimmy read Tolstoy, Twain, Shakespeare, and Joyce. Early on I thought it was for show, although I'm not sure whom there was to see. Anyway, I started picking up the books he was reading at the library and talking to him about them. I'm embarrassed to say his understanding was greater than mine in most cases. He would draw all kinds of parallels to other works of fiction, the Bible, fables, and even old movies.

The truth was, I found the man to be far more informed and interesting than the other guards. I came to look forward to our literary discussions and conversations regarding current events. But I can honestly say, I made an honest effort to never let myself get too close to Jimmy for two reasons. Number one, losing sight of the fact that Jimmy was a convicted killer could get me killed. While it was true that some of the Row inmates were not terrible bright, most were far more intelligent than your average inmate in gen pop, and, I dare say, the civilian population in general. And Jimmy was the brightest I'd ever met. If anyone could convince you in a million different ways of his innocence, it was Jimmy Bitz. The second reason I tried to keep him at a distance was because Jimmy, like the rest of the guys doing the Stretch, was scheduled to die soon by the authority vested in the state of New York.

As the date of an execution approached things changed on the Row. To say that death became palpable would probably be lost on all but those who had experienced war up close and personal. Inmates and staff alike would become tense as a sort of vicarious phenomenon gripped the place until the appointed hour had passed. Guards would go home more appreciative of their families and freedoms. Prisoners, I suspect, felt a part of themselves die with each execution and would be subdued for several days afterward, or at least until the recently vacated cell had been filled anew.

The appeals process kept things moving at a grinding pace, and the average time spent on the Row was around eighteen months. Individual emotions were like a roller coaster for some as a call from a lawyer could send one into the depths of despair. All too often, the most damning of things would enter the Row, but it never stayed long. Hope had a way of making falling feel like flying for a day or two. But the landings were never smooth.

Jimmy was as even keeled as could be. He had no lawyer and would only be disappointed at realizing he was smarter than his court appointed counsel anyway. If asked, and I did once, Jimmy would say that the good Lord had a plan for him. If not original, I figured it was as good a strategy and outlook as any, and let it go. All the same, I began to dread the day when his appointment with Big Surge would be made known.

I'd seen that announcement change a lot of men. Some stopped eating, some gave away what little they had, some picked up a Bible for the first time; some dropped it. Some became withdrawn, while others exhibited a false bravado during the day and could be heard weeping at night. It was hard to tell how a man might behave, but I likened it to the effect that whiskey has on men, amplifying their inner self. I couldn't predict how Jimmy would react any more than I knew tomorrow's lotto numbers.

Jimmy didn't change at all. Not his reading,

sleeping patterns, or demeanor. Same old Jimmy. It was the first day of December. I remember because the first and last piece of mail Jimmy ever received while at Sing Sing came that day, and it was a Christmas card. I handed him the envelope, which had no return address. "I thought you said you didn't have any family, Jimmy."

"I don't, Doc," Jimmy replied as if he got mail every day. He always called me Doc. I'm not sure why, but I didn't mind. I kind of think it was his way of telling me he regarded me as a bit more learned than the rest.

"Who then?" I inquired as he was opening it.

"Probably a lawyer," he said, and we both chuckled.

He held it up to his face like he did whenever he read. I could see the outside of the card. It was of the purest white cardstock, with an angel etched in red, I remember. Jimmy smiled and said simply, "Now isn't that nice."

I couldn't resist. "Who's it from?"

"None other than our Lord and Savior," Jimmy said, handing me the card.

Inside the card, in the same red etching was written:

Hebrews 5:7 *During the days of Jesus' life on earth, he offered up prayers and petitions with loud cries and tears to the one who could save him from death, and he was heard because of his reverent submission.*

There was no handwriting of at all. No signature. Nothing. I handed it back to Jimmy, and he took it to the back of his cell and stood it up on the small ledge above his sink. I remember thinking how it stood out like a beacon in that small, dark cell. Light at the end of a tunnel, as it were.

Jimmy Bitz was scheduled to die on January 1,

1973 at the stroke of midnight. I began to feel awkward around him, not knowing quite what to say. I stuck to the topic that had bound us. Literature was the place we both found most liberating when so much of my time, and all of his, was behind bars and concrete. We often mulled over our next selections, steering clear of the obvious (*Tale of Two Cities, As I Lay Dying,* etc.). Eventually, even this topic began to dry up. We had just started reading *Ivanhoe* when Jimmy began listing a few suggestions for our next book. I knew without looking at my watch that it was the twelfth of December. I knew that with roughly four hundred pages remaining, we would have to read better than fifty pages a day to finish the book before midnight of the new year's first day. Definitely doable but it stood to be our last book, just the same.

Jimmy sensed my apprehension and smiled, "We could probably squeeze in something short and sweet, maybe *The Red Pony* or *The Old Man and the Sea."*

I nodded, feeling my chest tighten. "Sure," I managed, realizing for the first time that I had failed to keep Jimmy at bay. I had broken my own rule. Always a staunch defender in capital punishment, I found myself chaffing at the senselessness of such a good mind being snuffed out.

That night after work, I stopped at the public library and after being assisted with the setup, began to pour over microfiche, which contained every article printed leading up to and during Jimmy's trial. There wasn't much, and what there was didn't deviate a whole lot from what Jimmy had told me. He readily admitted holding the bloody bat above the body when the other custodian walked in. The prosecutor claimed Jimmy bludgeoned Mary Ellen Hayes. Jimmy claimed he found the bat near her and made the mistake of picking it up. Driving home from the library, I realized I had wanted to find something that would convince me of Jimmy's guilt, something that would allow me to make sense of his execution. A sort of defense mechanism that would allow me to maintain my convictions regarding the death penalty and part with Jimmy emotionally unscathed.

Two days later, Jimmy greeted me with a grin. He held something behind his back. From any other prisoner I would have assumed a defensive posture, certain a bodily-fluid cocktail awaited me. With Jimmy, I was certain he had settled on a final reading. I also knew the book cart had been through the Row earlier in the day.

"Okay, what's it going to be?" I asked with reservation.

Jimmy proudly held up *A Christmas Carol* as though he had penned it himself. "I don't know why I didn't think of it sooner. It's the perfect book," he said.

And so it was. We raced through *Ivanhoe* in an effort to carve out a few days before the New Year. More than once I came to work exhausted, having only slept a few hours due to my late nigh reading. I read through lunches and breaks, in a dimly lit stairwell free of talk and cigarette smoke.

We began Dickens's carol on the twenty-ninth. The three days prior to any execution afforded the inmate nearing the end of the Stretch any number of opportunities to accept visitors. The visitations usually consisted of family members, lawyers selling hope in small doses, and clergy. Jimmy received none of these, only asking that I join him in the reading of man's second most revered Christmas miracle.

I was given permission to spend the time with the condemned man, suffering no loss of vacation time or pay. I sat on a small stool facing Jimmy, who sat on the edge of his bunk so tightly made, a staff sergeant would have approved. We each had a copy of the small book and took turns reading passages. When it came to dialogue between Scrooge and a Ghost, Jimmy and I would engage in a similar division of labor, with me usually assuming the voice of dear old Ebenezer.

After a passage involving the recognition of some regrets on Scrooge's part, Jimmy asked me if I had any regrets. I told him that I had wanted to be an English teacher but that after leaving the service I felt more suited to the line of work in which I presently found myself. He was quiet, and I realized he wanted me to ask the same of him.

When I did so he said sadly, "My only regret involves the two children my wife and I lost in childbirth." Before I could express my sympathy Jimmy continued, "The second one took my wife, too. She had been afraid to try again after the first. I pushed her. Wanted a child so badly." A large, solitary tear dropped onto the illustration of Tiny Tim atop Bob Cratchit's shoulders.

"I had no idea," was all I could muster.

Driving home in silence that night, I realized that in addition to telling me of the sadness that had defined much of his life, Jimmy had for the final time, told me of his innocence regarding Mary Ellen Hayes. I also realized that I now believed him.

In a departure from our earlier roles, Jimmy read the part of Scrooge as the old skinflint sought to gain understanding from the Ghost of Christmas

Future. With great conviction and feeling Jimmy begged the spirit to tell him if he still had time to change his miserly ways.

I was to read the following line as the narrator and found myself unable. Instead, before I could stop myself I asked, "Do you share his fear regarding the unknown?" I was in earnest, like a child seeking reassurance from a parent.

Jimmy, brought back from gazing at Scrooge's tombstone amidst a dark cemetery in nineteenth century London, settled his eyes on me. "I would if it *were* unknown," he said with a sincerity rarely seen inside those thick walls. "I *know* where I'm going, Doc."

I left that night convinced he did, having gotten the reassurance I had sought.

The day of an execution is one in which the famous last meal is given. The prisoner is isolated in a windowless room with only one door and a guard posted. Last rites are administered, and in the movies a good deal of emphasis is placed on the possibility involving a last minute phone call from the governor. Jimmy did request a meal and addressed it like any other. That morning he had also accepted the last rites of a clergyman he had politely declined to see previously. No mention was made of the governor, however.

Instead, Jimmy and I read the final stave of Dickens's masterpiece with Jimmy hugging the open book to his chest and closing his eyes as he blissfully uttered the final words, "*God bless Us, Every One*."

For days I had put off asking him if he wanted me to attend his execution. I surely would have done it but hoped he would spare me the experience. How funny that sentence reads. I was certain he would bring it up if it were important to him. With only a few moments left before I had to leave, I finally asked him. I'll never forget his response, which turned out to be our parting words. He shook my hand warmly, a sincere, meaningful, two-hand shake and said simply, "I don't think it will come to that, Doc."

It did not. I was standing over a sink, looking in the mirror of the break room wishing it were a year later, when undoubtedly my nerves would no longer be raw and frayed. The cold water I had splashed on my face had finished dripping into the sink when Ralph Peterson opened the door in a panic. "Missing prisoner! We may have an escape! All hands. All hands."

I asked whom, even though I knew.

The Row was essentially a long corridor with cells lining the south wall. At one end of the corridor was the office, or control room, equipped with screens showing the corridor from each end. A third screen showed the platform outside the office so that anyone gaining admittance into the Row could be seen by the officer hitting the button to activate the electric door. A locked cabinet contained several riot shotguns and a supply of shot shells and beanbags. A steel door at the other end of the Row opened to a twenty-four foot, narrow hall with a solid door on each side. On the north side was the staff locker room, which doubled as a break room. Jimmy had been in the isolation room on the south side. Neither room had any windows.

Perry Stephens had been guarding the door. We had acknowledged each other by nodding our heads grimly as I left the room after saying my good-byes to Jimmy. Lou Bingham had been in the control room, while Ralph had been walking the line. Ralph and I raced through the Row and joined Perry and Lou in the control room. Perry was as white as a ghost. Lou was studying the log, which indicates whom and when someone enters the Row through the office. A record is kept digitally when the override is pressed activating the electric door. Lou kept staring at the number, which read like an alarm clock with big red digital letters. The four of us had started our shift at two, and the number 2:04 was the last time the door had opened, allowing the crew we replaced to leave. It had not been opened since.

I had left Jimmy at six when Perry had brought in his last meal. It was now nearing seven thirty. Jimmy's date with Big Surge was less than five hours away. Jimmy had been in the isolation room since noon. It took less than an hour to scour the place under the guise of a contraband search. The inmates, already on edge, didn't appreciate the search in the least but were powerless to stop it. Each locker was opened; the toilet in the break room was examined; under each bunk was searched. All in vain. Jimmy Bitz had disappeared into thin air.

We could no longer put off calling Warden Rafer, who showed up red-faced and accompanied by an assistant not more than five minutes later. He demanded that Lou show him the digital readout of the entry portal. Rafer then asked when we had each seen Bitz. He studied us each piercingly as we responded, as if he could root out a liar with his gaze. Protocol dictated that the entire facility be placed under lockdown immediately.

I knew this would be a night unlike any other when Rafer, rather than order the lockdown, sat at the table and insisted we do the same. It soon became apparent that in the seven minutes since he'd received the phone call, Warden Rafer had determined that under no circumstances would the institution acknowledge that Jimmy Bitz had escaped, even if Jimmy Bitz *had* escaped.

That night, at precisely eleven thirty, Paul, Lou, and I walked out of the isolation room flanking an inmate who was dressed in prison attire and handcuffed. He was holding a newspaper over his face as if avoiding photographers. If the inmates suspected shame was the cause of his face being covered they were more right than they could have imagined. Behind that morning's edition of the Post, Perry Stephens was every bit as ashamed as Lou, Paul, and myself.

As strange as Jimmy's disappearance was, even stranger was Warden Rafer's handling of the situation. After proposing what I regarded as preposterous, the Warden assured us that there had been no applications to witness the execution. Jimmy had no family, and the press had grown mostly disinterested due to the high volume of executions during the past two years. Mary Ellen Hayes had family but evidently none who were interested in seeing Jimmy Bitz die up close and personal. Since the only people witnessing the execution were those administering it, Rafer convinced us we could go through the motions as if it were conducted legitimately.

I couldn't believe what I was hearing. It was like the *Twilight Zone*. I looked around the table at Lou, Paul, and Perry who were all clearly loving the idea, since it involved keeping their jobs. I asked about the presence of a doctor and was introduced to Warden Rafer's assistant who was evidently credentialed as such.

"What do we do in a week or two when Jimmy Bitz shows up in Boston, Philly, or even Miami?" I asked incredulously. The looks on my fellow guards suggested that this hadn't crossed their minds. They looked hopefully at the warden.

Talk about hearing a pin drop. Warden Rafer leaned toward the center of the table and whispered with the conviction of a man who'd bet his very life, "He won't. I guarantee it."

I didn't sleep at all that night wondering about a great many things. I wondered how the warden could guarantee such a thing. I wondered how he could expect five guys, if you counted his assistant, to keep a secret. I wondered what would happen when the truth came out. I wondered where Jimmy Bitz was that night. I wondered what Jimmy had known or meant when he said, *I don't think it will come to that, Doc.*

I came in the next day even though I wasn't scheduled to work. Among the things that had floated in my mind during the sleepless night had been the card Jimmy had gotten in the mail. I don't know why, but I wanted to see it again for myself. I cleaned out his cell, removing all personal items. Other than some toiletries and Bible, the brilliantly white card was all he left behind. I looked it over for any indication of whom it was from or even where it was purchased. The back of every card I had ever seen has small print, usually indicating something proprietary regarding Hallmark. This card had nothing.

Two days later, I found myself summoned to Warden Rafer's office following the conclusion of my shift. I was asked to sit at one of the two chairs in front of Rafer's desk. Occupying the other was Rafer's assistant. With very little fanfare I was shown a document, which amounted to an early retirement agreement. I was told that despite having three years to go before becoming eligible for a pension, I would be accorded such a status effective immediately following the drying of my signature on said document. I asked why this offer was being made.

"We're looking to make some procedural changes in terms of the day-to-day operations on the Row, so as to insure that events of the past week don't repeat themselves," the Warden said, hands folded on his immaculate desk. "We're going to start with a fresh batch of guards and train them utilizing the new procedures. No old habits."

"Are you offering Peterson, Bingham, and Stephens early retirement too? Stephens is only twenty-seven years old," I asked, baffled by what I was hearing.

"They've all been transferred to other facilities," Rafer said calmly.

I looked out the warden's window. The bare trees were blowing in the wind, and the sky was grey. "I don't know what to make of this," I said. "Do I have a few days to think it over?"

"We need your signature today," Rafer's assistant broke in, speaking for the first time.

"Let me get this straight. I sign and get a full pension check starting next month?" I asked, certain I was missing something.

"It's that simple," the warden said, smiling.

"Not quite," Rafer's assistant said, pursing his lips.

Warden Rafer stopped smiling and turned to the last page of the document before us. "There is a confidentiality agreement you'll need to sign as part of the deal."

I leaned back in my chair as things began to make sense. "You want to make sure I don't blab to the press about Jimmy's escape."

"Or to anyone else. Ever." Warden Rafer leaned across his desk and stared me straight in the eyes. "If you ever speak of this matter to another living soul from this moment forward, your pension will stop, and efforts will be made to recover monies already paid out."

"Whether you are alive or not," the assistant added ominously.

I couldn't tell whether my life was being threatened, or they were threatening to throw my wife out on the street should she outlive me. It could have been both. There was silence in the room, and I could remember taking a business class in college where the instructor had mentioned the point in a sales call where it became a matter of the next person to speak losing. The thing was, I couldn't see losing anything by signing. It seemed like a win for everyone but the taxpayer. So, I signed.

I've often wondered what would have happened had I refused to take the pension. The truth was, I suspect, that I would have lost my stomach for the job if they really had executed Jimmy Bitz. I had no proof, but I was sure the man was innocent. Just a gut feeling, I guess. I spent the following days tempted to pay Paul or Lou a home visit. I drove by Lou's house, and there was a moving van out front. I went for coffee and mulled going back and offering a hand with the moving. That didn't break the agreement. I didn't have to broach the subject to lend a hand to an old friend. I drove back and found the van was gone and the house empty.

So there I was, forty-seven years old, retired, and looking at a whole lot of time on my hands. Mark graduated that spring, and your mother and I decided to downsize. That was when we moved to Akron, where I got my job teaching lit at a private school. Some of the best moments of my life came each December, reading *A Christmas Carol* with my classes. I can still hear Jimmy blissfully end the story, eyes closed, *God Bless Us, Every One!*

Years passed, and while I thought of Jimmy often, I came to accept that his disappearance was one of life's many mysteries that I would never solve. Sometimes I thought I dreamed it all. Sometimes I thought it happened just to nudge me into pursuing the teaching I so enjoyed. I often thought how much like a Dickens's novel it would be to have Jimmy approach me on the street some day.

It never happened, though. Instead, as you know, I became obsessed with the Edward Milton case. Advances in forensics had determined that Milton could not have even been at the scene of the murder for which he had been convicted. The anti-death penalty people went crazy. The first confirmed case of an innocent man having been put to death was the talk of the nation for weeks before another crises crowded it out of the headlines. It may have drifted from my mind too, except that Milton, who had been put to death thirty-three years earlier, was executed at Sing Sing, during Bill Rafer's first year as warden.

It was around that time that I decided to retire from teaching. Your mother and I were back in Ossining visiting her family when I took an afternoon to look up an old friend. Earl Flagg had been an old-timer when I first came to D Block. He had done time on the Row and found he took too much home in his head at night. Earl transferred to D Block, where hope, he said, wasn't entirely extinguished. I had learned a lot from Earl, including the fact that a small measure of humanity still remained in each inmate; regardless of how much they wanted to convince you otherwise.

Sitting on Earl's front porch drinking lemonade, we talked about how penology had changed, budgets cuts endangered staff, and how the world seemed to be going to hell in a hand basket. I told Earl I would have been shived several times if it hadn't been for his sagacious advice, taking me under his wing the way he had. He chuckled modestly, and I asked him if he'd had the benefit of an older guard when he had started out.

"No. Not really that I can recall. Most of the older guys in those days were real hard asses. Treated the new guards little better than the prisoners until they'd been around for a while," Earl mused.

"You remember any of their names?" I asked, trying to sound casual.

"Why?" Earl was old, but not stupid.

"I was just wondering if they were any of the guys my uncle worked with," I said.

"Your uncle work the Row?" Earl asked, surprised.

"Short stint." I hated to lie, but I needed some names.

Earl relaxed, sipped from his lemonade and tilted his head back. "Let's see now. There was Dick Reeves and John Stinson. Course John's dead now."

Dick Reeves was too, it turned out. His wife told me he'd died just a year before, when I looked up his address and came by their home shortly after my conversation with Earl. The widow, Reeves, mentioned another name when prompted. She seemed so grateful to have a visitor she never even asked why I'd come by. The name Mrs. Reeves gave me was that of Donald Kowalski. After a brief visit with his daughter, I found Donald where she said I might.

Donald Kowalski was the man that is seen in every park that sports a pond with ducks and geese. He's that old man who spends his days throwing pieces of bread or popcorn out of a brown lunch sack at fowl that think he's a godsend. I am able to identify that old man now because I have become him. At any rate, I joined him on his bench after asking if the seat was taken. He shrugged, having heard stupid questions before, I'm sure.

Having seen Donald from across the pond, I had purchased a bag of popcorn from a vendor before making my way over. The way Donald called the ducks by name before throwing their way, made it clear that this was how he spent a good deal of each day. I was new and therefore breaking into his routine.

"Retirement's golden," I commented, throwing my first piece of popcorn. Donald said nothing, and I wasn't certain he had heard me. "You have a name for each bird?" I asked, trying again.

"Maybe," Donald answered, eyes still on his flock.

"I just retired," I said truthfully.

"Welcome to the party," Donald said dryly.

"I was a teacher," I said, hoping Donald would reciprocate.

"Kids these days," he said, as if expected to say just that.

"Yeah. They're something. You been retired long?" I asked.

"About twenty years," Kowalski replied.

"Yeah? What'd you do?" I prompted.

"Security." Donald tossed a piece of bread to a mallard in the back.

"Like prison?" I asked innocently.

Donald looked at me for the first time. "Like a warehouse."

"Oh, right," I responded. "I worked in a prison once."

"Thought you said you was a teacher." Donald was still eyeing me.

"Yeah. I was, but I worked in a prison before that," I said, appreciating the ability to stay in the same zip code as the truth.

Donald was quiet. He proceeded to feed the birds, but his brow was wrinkled now. After five minutes or so, he spoke again. "I actually worked in a prison for a short time myself," he said finally.

I just nodded as if no longer interested, hoping Donald would continue. He didn't, but his brow remained furrowed. "Yeah, it's not for everyone," I finally said. Donald nodded again. "Security pay a lot better?" I asked.

"Not really. I only left because I got canned," Donald said. I looked at him puzzled, imploring him with my eyes to continue. The old man looked at me, shrugged his shoulders and said simply, "Prisoner escaped on my watch." As he said this, Donald's eyes darted, scanning the park.

"Minimum security?" I asked, as if I didn't know.

"Maximum," Donald sighed.

"You fall asleep?"

"Hell no," Donald said defensively.

"So what happened?"

Donald scattered the small crumbs from the bottom of his bag to the birds that became briefly frenzied. He crumpled the bag into a small brown ball and placed it on the bench between us. I could tell he was deciding whether or not to tell the story behind his firing, the story I had come to hear. He took a small silver flask out of a jacket pocket and unscrewed the lid before taking a slug. He didn't offer it to me, as I feared he might.

"You don't fall asleep when an inmate is about to be executed. You don't even sleep that night when you go home." Donald took another slug before continuing, "And when you do finally fall asleep, let me tell ya, it's not the same sleep you enjoyed before your first execution." Donald stopped, and I could tell he was weighing the benefits of continuing. I could also sense he wanted to get something off his chest.

"I'll bet," I said, hoping I didn't sound as fake as I felt.

A third swig prompted Donald to go on. "Fellow whose Stretch was nearly done was a hateful man. Bitter, angry, and full of hate. Said all along that he was innocent and had been railroaded. Said he wished he *had* killed the man he was convicted of murdering. Kept to himself, never talked to the other inmates. Called 'em criminals." This caused Donald to laugh bitterly. "Of course Milton hated the guards too." Donald took another sip.

"Did you say Milton? Didn't I just read about him? There was a Milton in the papers not too long ago," I urged.

Donald took a long pull from his flask. "Yeah. Same guy. First innocent man to have been executed." I sat spellbound. "Except he wasn't," the former guard added, almost as an afterthought.

"Innocent?" I managed.

"Executed."

"I don't follow," I said.

"He escaped," Donald explained.

"He escaped?" I repeated dumbfounded.

"I suppose so," Donald said, staring out over the pond in sad resignation.

"What do you mean?" I asked in anticipation.

"I mean he disappeared," Donald said vacantly.

"Disappeared?" It was what I had anticipated, but now that I was hearing it the claim seemed impossible to believe.

"Clergy came in the morning to give him his last rites. Milton refused and gave the man a good cussing. So he left. I went to check on Milton ten minutes later, and he was gone."

"Gone?" I asked, still unsure of what I was hearing.

"Gone. His cell door was still locked. We searched his cell. No tunnel, no nothing. The man just plain disappeared."

"So how come the papers say he was executed?" I returned.

"They say they found him," Donald said, clearly not convinced.

"Did you see him again?"

"No. The warden fired me and another guy who was on duty at the time. We were told to clear out immediately," Donald answered.

"You don't think they found him?" I asked, needing convincing.

"Nah. I think they probably executed a dead man."

"A dead man? Why do you think that?" I asked genuinely confused.

Donald took another long pull on his nearly empty flask. "Two reasons. One, there was a fatal stabbing in the yard later in the day." Donald looked at me, and I could see more than bloodshot in his eyes. "Two; Milton's mother was the only witness."

"So?" I pleaded.

"So she got rear ended in the parking lot by a prison van. Didn't get up to the gallery until they'd already put the bag over her boy's head."

I'll be the first to admit I became a bit obsessed after that. I'd like to say it was because I wanted to clear Jimmy's name, but the truth is, no one cared. He didn't have any kin, and the public couldn't care less. Warden Rafer's dead, and while he was guilty of a cover-up, it's not like he killed these men. Hell, just the opposite; it was his job to kill them, and he didn't. I guess my views on capital punishment have changed somewhat, though. I'm not against putting to death an individual who murdered another. But given that the system is run by imperfect people who I'm convinced have erred on numerous occasions, I'm not sure capital punishment is one for men to administer.

I think in an odd way this odyssey of sorts was my seeking an answer regarding a higher power. I'd grown up going to church, praying before meals and bedtime. I'd gone through the motions like I imagine so many do. I don't know that I gave it any real thought or examination. But there comes a time when you see your parents dying off that you realize your generation is next to walk life's plank. Going through the motions doesn't cut it any more. You have to know. At least I did. Faith is a beautiful thing, but it comes easier for some than others. I had to be shown in order to believe. I guess it's that hardheaded Irish in me.

Spending hour after hour looking at that flimsy Bitz file left me with only one avenue. I went to see the man who had come upon Jimmy holding the bat. The nursing home I found Ray Thomas in was almost certainly his last stop. The man was thin and pale with skin that betrayed a life long smoker. He perspired in the shade and couldn't stand the sun. He was clearly sick and on the last leg of life's journey.

I joined him at a table where he sat in his wheel chair alone, eating cottage cheese and peaches from a plastic fork. I introduced myself but didn't give any background. When he asked if I was a reporter I told him the truth; I was just an old friend of Jimmy's. He became withdrawn, and I left after he signaled a young attendant to take him back to his room.

The next time I came to visit Ray I brought a cribbage board and didn't mention Jimmy once. He said he didn't play and eyed me suspiciously while I dealt. Three fives helped jog his memory, and we began to play. Ray didn't get any visitors in the six weeks we played cards. He'd just turn off the television with his remote and clear a space on his small table when I walked into the room he shared with another gentleman who was rarely visible from the other side of a curtain.

When the weather was nice I'd wheel him out, and we'd play on a picnic table in a small courtyard. One day, after double skunking me, he told me he was dying.

"I know," I replied quietly, shuffling the cards and restoring the pegs.

"What do you want from me?" he asked.

"I'd start with getting my dollar back," I replied.

Ray smiled, relieved at my levity. Before I left that day I said, "You'll tell me when you're ready, Ray. See you tomorrow."

Three days later Ray asked that I wheel him outside to play. I told him that I thought it was a bit cold, but he didn't care. I wrapped a blanket around his shoulders and wheeled him out. We had the courtyard to ourselves, which was the way Ray wanted it. I took the deck of cards out of my pocket and began to deal. Ray was quiet and subdued. I asked him how he was feeling.

"Guilty," was his reply.

I tossed two cards in the crib and waited for him to discard a burden he'd been carrying for nearly half a century.

"Ms. Hayes caught me going through the school safe a few weeks before it happened," Ray said, placing his cards down. "I begged her not to tell anyone."

I put my cards down and folded my hands. "Did she?" I asked.

"No but every time I saw her she'd joke about it. Like it was some kind of game to her. Said she wanted her room waxed, special. Stuff like that," Ray continued.

"So you finally had enough?" I inquired gently.

"Yeah. When she told me there was a bunch of fundraising money in the safe and that she wanted me to get it for her. I knew this was never going to end. She'd hold this over me forever," Ray said glumly. "I wasn't trying to frame Jimmy. Poor bastard was there a half hour early." Ray began to convulse, and he put his hands to his face to hide his shame.

I put my hand on his shoulder, and he looked up and asked, "Do you think God can forgive me?"

"I think God can do anything," I said honestly.

"I can live with what I did to Ms. Hayes. I really can. But getting Jimmy killed is unforgivable," Ray choked.

I didn't know what to say, so I repeated

myself. “I think God can do anything, Ray.”

And I still do. Which is why I’ve written this all down for you boys. I don’t expect this to embolden you with religious fervor. As I said before, religion is a highly personal matter and a journey I imagine each of us has to make on our own. I only hope that my experience will serve to open your eyes to the possibility that God exists.

Mark Collins stood in the dark, admiring the house from the street while light snowfall graced his face. It reminded him of a Christmas card: the perfect two-story house with bright lights hanging from the eves, a snowman out front and a wreath on the door. Mark walked up to the door, rang the bell, and stood with two packages under his arms and his heart aflutter. Tom Collins answered the door and stood in shock for a moment before welcoming him in.

Several hours later, as the brothers were talking quietly at the kitchen table, Tom’s son, David, came into the room for a glass of milk before bed. Mark sat him on his lap while Tom got up to get the milk. David was holding his grandfather’s notebook as Mark bounced the boy on his knee. An envelope addressed to John Collins, fell out of the notebook and onto the floor. The envelope had no return address and was postmarked April 11, 1999. Inside was found a card of the whitest paper either man had ever seen.

Wish of the Kept

The halls of a hospital late at night are almost surreal. They are quiet, lit in a way that is strangely neither warm nor cold, and they are often timeless despite a clock finishing every corridor like the punctuation of a sentence. Time is visible but fails to register in the minds of those traipsing through from the parking lot to a loved one's rooms, vice versa, or more likely, to or from the cafeteria in search of mediocre coffee or a temporary respite from the anguish involved with watching familial withering. The initial odor, cleaning agent, or was it faintly medicinal, has long since faded from the perception of the frequent visitor who could find the room they seek blindfolded but couldn't direct another for some inexplicable reason no doubt pertaining to the burden carried both coming and going.

In hospitals with some religious affiliation, statues the sizes of small children often adorn hollowed alcoves near elevators. They are nearly always accompanied with a plaque commemorating at least one beloved, if not generous, benefactor. These statues bask under a warm glow provided by canned lighting and more often than not resemble the Virgin Mary. Those affected by the sight of these statues have typically one of two reactions. Many are angered and bitter, doubting God's very existence, or feeling as if God has shunned or punished their families in spite of innumerable pleas for help. More often than not, though, people choose to be reminded that miracles are a part of life's mysteries and like lottery tickets, represent hope for many a downtrodden.

Kevin Steele waited for the elevator to open, a Styrofoam cup of coffee in one hand and hot cocoa in the other. The late night quiet disturbed only by the gentle humming and muted clicking of the elevator's workings behind the closed well-polished stainless steel sliding doors. Kevin sensed the presence of another and looked to his left, seeing only the statue of Mary. He smiled faintly at the statue, aware of a curious co-mingling of bitterness and hope as the doors in front of him parted with a ding.

Outside of room 442, Kevin turned his shoulder toward the door and took a deep breath, bracing himself before shouldering it open. Despite spending the past three weeks at his son's bedside, re-entering the room always forced the air from Kevin's lungs. He would never get used to seeing tubes coming from Kenny's arms or nose. Tubes attached to machines with green and red lights dictating the stop and go of Kenny's internal systems. Just the stillness with which his son lay was unsettling, as Kevin had always marveled at the boy's boundless energy until he had fallen ill.

Placing the two cups on Kenny's sliding tray, Kevin felt his son's forehead and brushed the sandy brown hair from Kenny's closed eyes. The boy was sleeping shallowly, judging from the faint breathing and mist of sweat on cheeks preternaturally red. Kevin wet a washcloth from a water bottle and dabbed lightly at Kenny's forehead before sitting down in the soft-bottomed but hard-armed chair next to the hospital bed. Kevin felt a pang in his stomach reminding him of the sandwich he had not eaten but had promised his wife he would.

Anna Steele had taken the diagnosis with a determined stride. Her faith had not wavered, even as Kenny's prognosis had worsened. She had realized almost immediately that her strength was needed in order to keep Kevin above water. It wasn't that her husband was weak. Far from it. But Anna knew her husband had two strikes against him from the get-go. Kevin had been serving as the man of the family, holding strong for his mother and younger brother for more than a decade before Anna had met him. As a twelve year old Kevin had watched his father stricken and decay at the hands of the same insidious disease that now gripped their son.

Kevin had seen a strong and virile man fade before his eyes while telling his son repeatedly that everything would be all right. It hadn't been all right, though, as Kevin found the supposedly carefree joys of his teen years dampened by a blanket or lens that made his outlook darker and more somber than that of his peers. It forever altered the relationship with his brother Robert, two years his junior. Kevin always on Robert about staying on the straight and narrow, both elusive to the younger Steele. Robert's wayward ways weighed on Kevin, who took it to heart as a failure on his own part.

Despite the doctors' insistence that the disease was not hereditary, Anna knew that Kevin blamed himself for their son's malady, as if he had provided a bridge for the disease to move from his father to his son. It was this she saw in her husband's face as he leaned over Kenny's hospital bed for the first time and ever since. She couldn't tell if it was just stress or a form of self-punishment, but Kevin rarely ate now and had shed weight he could hardly afford.

Kevin sat in the near dark holding both cups, taking a sip from one and carefully displacing it with the other so that gradually both held a mix of hot chocolate and coffee. He put his feet up on one of the struts that formed the mobile frame of Kenny's hospital bed and leaned back in a position that he'd spent most nights of late. The stillness of the hour allowed him to reflect on a similar situation two decades prior. The unfairness of it had overwhelmed him then and was threatening to do so again. Kevin's father had made all the right decisions, stayed out of trouble, worked hard, married well, and could look forward to seeing his sons grow up into responsible young men that would perhaps someday, give him grandchildren who would contribute immeasurably to his golden years. In the prime of life, though, this dream of seeing the fruits of his labors realized had been snatched from him. Kevin could make no sense of it then, and the time since had yielded little or nothing in the direction of reason.

But this illness coming back for Kenny was even less comprehensible. For years, Kevin had feared a similar fate to that of his father. With his last birthday, Kevin had eclipsed the age at which his father had succumbed to the disease, and his fear had gradually begun to wane. Until now. This was worse. Losing Kenny would be worse than having the disease come for him. Of this, Kevin was certain.

And so, it was with a measure of desperation that Kevin found himself kneeling on the floor at the side of Kenny's bed. He clasped his hands, bowed his head, and began to issue prayer and tears without inhibition. It had been two decades since he'd last spoken to God, and the desperate man knew well the hypocrisy involved with coming to God only when in need and as a last resort, but he didn't care. What had he to lose that he wasn't already losing day-by-day, blood count by count?

Like so many through the years who had faced

pending loss, Kevin promised he would be a new man, go to church, and pray to God regularly, if only his son were spared. Baring his soul and no longer questioning why this was happening, Kevin sought only a relinquishment in the condition that gripped his boy. With sincerity only a parent can voice, Kevin begged that it be he who carried the burden of the disease, rather than his son. All this and more Kevin effused as a small puddle of tears pooled beneath the bed that held a boy doctors had given less than a month to live. With his tears all but exhausted in a final plea reiterating his desire to absorb the burden carried by his son, Kevin sat back in the chair, pulled his coat over his core and closed his still-wet eyes.

The next morning, when Kevin returned home for a shower and book to read to Kenny, he found his brother asleep on the couch in the living room. Anna, wearing a thick bathrobe, was seated at the kitchen table with a cup of coffee and the morning paper. She raised a knowing eyebrow as Kevin approached asking, "What's he doing here?"

"Wanted to see Kenny," Anna answered. "I told him he could use the guest room after I clean it."

"When did he get here?" Kevin asked skeptically.

"Late," Anna answered evenly.

"Was he sober?"

Anna put down her coffee. "Does it matter?" she responded.

"Was he?" Kevin repeated.

Anna reached for her husband's hand. "He's your brother, Kevin."

Kevin pulled his hand away. "I don't want him around Kenny if he's using again."

Anna got up and went into the kitchen, coming

back with a cup of coffee for Kevin who had sat at the table, putting his weary face in his hands. She placed the cup beside him and stood behind him rubbing her husband's shoulders. "I don't know. I didn't ask, and he didn't say."

Kevin rubbed his temples as if he could pre-empt the headache he felt coming on. "I don't want him around if he's doing drugs," he repeated unevenly as Anna's hands found a knot in his back.

"You know how much Kenny loves Robert," Anna said carefully. "It'd do Kenny good to see his uncle."

"Not if his uncle is high," Kevin retorted, knowing all the while that Anna was right.

Anna's response was measured. "This can't be easy on Robert, you know."

"Why are you always defending him, taking his side?" Kevin implored, pointing toward the couch.

Anna pulled her chair close to Kevin's and held both his hands in hers as she leaned close to him. "There are no sides. We are a family who is experiencing something terrible. Something no family should have to endure. We need to lean on one another. Robert may be a grown man, but he still needs you. You've always been a source of strength to him."

Through bloodshot eyes Kevin whispered, "I'm tired of being my brother's keeper. Maybe *I* don't have any strength left. Maybe it's all gone."

Anna smiled and caressed his cheek. "I don't believe that. I think you have enough for Kenny *and* Robert."

Kevin looked into his wife's eyes and discerned that she was telling the truth. He wondered for a moment what he ever did to deserve her. The moment was short-lived, as the figure on their couch began to turn, knocking over an empty milk glass on the coffee table. It clattered loudly, bringing a laugh from Anna who stood up. "I'll make you two breakfast," she said cheerfully. "And you be good to your brother," Anna mouthed to her husband.

Kevin took the coffee Anna had brought him into the living room. He looked down at the form on his couch. The familiar and worn green Army jacket, which always smelled as if his father had put it away moist before Robert had discovered it years later, was strewn on the floor by the couch. Robert's hair was stringy, dirty, and in need of cutting. His complexion was pale and poor with the skin on his thin arms revealing veins close to the surface. Kevin looked for needle marks he'd seen in the past and was grateful to see no such evidence. He sat down gently on Robert's feet. Robert stirred, looked at him through his disheveled mop of hair and pulled his feet free while clutching a comforter to his chin.

"Morning sunshine," Kevin said while extending the mug to his brother who warily reached out from under the comforter and grasped the handle.

"Morning," Robert returned, sitting up and leaning the small of his back against the arm of the couch.

"What brings you our way?" Kevin asked, trying to sound more casual than judgmental.

"Anna said," With this, Robert was overtaken with a bout of coughing that turned him red in the face.

"You okay?" Kevin offered.

Robert ignored him and recovered to finish his sentence. "Anna said Kenny's not doing so great."

Kevin nodded grimly. "Doctors say his counts are worsening."

"So what can they do?" Robert asked.

"I don't know. He's still so weak from the last treatment, " Kevin replied.

"Have you talked to other..," Robert began to cough violently again.

Kevin winced and waited for his brother's coughing to subside. "You might want to give up the smokes, Robert."

Robert regained his composure and sipped deeply from the mug before responding, "Gave 'em up five months ago, Kevin."

Kevin looked his brother in the eyes and thought better of challenging him on an assertion he seriously doubted. Instead, he smiled weakly and merely nodded.

After breakfast and showers, Kevin and Robert drove to the hospital in an awkward quiet, Kevin hoping the eggshells on which he was treading would remain unbroken if he remained silent. When they arrived, Kenny was awake, starring at a muted television mounted in a corner of his room. The boy broke into a smile upon seeing his uncle, who immediately produced a shiny red Matchbox car from a pocket in his Army jacket.

"A Cobra!" The boy said in delight as he struggled weakly to sit up.

"You know it, baby," Robert said handing it to his nephew. "Just like the one I'll buy you when I win the lottery." Robert sat on the side of the bed and tussled Kenny's damp hair. Kevin bit his tongue seeing the first joy in his son's eyes in nearly a month. "Your mom and dad tell me you're not feeling so hot lately, but you don't look so bad to me."

"I'm actually feeling a little better today," Kenny said bravely.

"Of course you are. That's cause your uncle

Bobby's in town. We'll get you back on your feet in no time," Robert added enthusiastically.

Kenny glanced doubtfully toward his father who tried to smile and then back to his uncle. "Do you really think I'll get better, Uncle Bobby?"

Kevin bit his lip as Robert turned to him and then back to the boy. "I know you will," Robert declared confidently.

"Really?" Kenny asked, brightening visibly.

Robert held up three fingers as if making a Scout's oath. "I promise."

Kevin lit into his brother as soon as the elevator door had shut. "Where do you get off on making a promise like that?" he growled just inches from Robert's face.

Robert looked startled and backed into the elevator wall. "I don't know. I just believe it. I really do."

"Based on what, your many years of medical school? Oh no, I forgot, you dropped out of high school to pursue a career in pharmacy." Kevin turned and faced the front of the elevator, looking at the backlit numbers above the door so as to avoid looking at this brother.

The elevator stopped. "Jesus, dude. Lighten up. Have a little faith." Robert said and walked out of the elevator.

The tension between the brothers was melted by news of progressively positive blood counts two days later. Kenny's energy returned, and it became impossible to keep him in his room much less his bed as he made his way into the halls in order to provide wide open spaces for the Cobra to roam. Befuddled doctors began to talk of remission while nurses murmured of miracles. Within a week Kenny was released to go home with orders, accompanied by winks, to take it easy.

Several nights later, still celebrating Kenny's release, the family enjoyed pizza, root beer and video games at Kenny's favorite restaurant. Kenny and Robert were playing a pinball machine while Kevin and Anna waited at their table for the pizza to arrive. Robert was doing his best not to let his nephew beat him, and Kenny was doing his best to make it look like a close match so as not to discourage his uncle.

"How'd you know I was going to get better?" The boy asked.

"Power of positive thinking, my man," Robert replied, concentrating on timing the flippers to maximize their striking power.

Kenny pondered this a moment, took a turn that was uncharacteristically short, and finally commented, "My dad didn't think I was going to get better."

"Sure he did."

"No he didn't," Kenny said flatly.

The lanky man turned to his nephew, letting the pinball past his defenses and got on one knee so that his eyes were level with his kin. "Don't get down on your old man. He watched our father die of the same thing. You can't blame him for being scared."

"I know. But-"

"But nothing. He loves you more than anything, and you're lucky to have him for your dad," Robert returned sharply.

"If that's how you feel, how come you guys always fight?" Kenny asked impudently.

Robert stood up and dropped another quarter into the machine, his shoulders slumping a bit. "It's complicated." There was no response from the boy who stood still, refusing to be placated by what he regarded as an inadequate response to his question. "Can't we just play?" Robert asked mildly irritated, sensing Kenny's unsatisfied stare. Kenny merely shook his head.

"Your dad's always wanted me to live a certain way," Robert began as the machine lit up once more. "He's always tried to keep me from making mistakes. But I just had to live life my own way," Robert said with a tinge of regret. "I'm not like him. I wish I were, but I'm not."

The air seemed to leave the room after this, and the lively music piped in through speakers in the ceiling stopped as a song ended. Kenny looked at his uncle who suddenly seemed both sad and older. "That's OK. I guess brothers are supposed to fight sometimes," he said.

"Yeah, maybe," Robert said, seemingly relieved. "But don't think for a minute I don't love your dad." Kenny smiled and another song began. Beeping sounds accompanied flashing lights as the machine registered Robert's score. "I'd do anything for the guy," he finished, as much to himself as his nephew.

Kevin and Anna sat in the booth watching Robert and Kenny. Anna moved closer and leaned her head on Kevin's shoulder. "I wonder what they're talking about," Anna mused.

"I'm not sure I want to know," Kevin answered, sipping root beer from a mug.

"Kenny really looks up to him you know."

"That's what I'm afraid of," Kevin scoffed.

"I don't think he's using. He said he quit smoking almost six months ago. That says something," Anna insisted.

"Yeah, maybe. He still looks like hell," Kevin countered.

Anna could think of nothing to say to that and had to admit to herself that Robert had continued to look thin, pale, and tired even after Kenny's recovery. Kevin's appetite, however, had returned with a vengeance, and he looked better already.

"Looks like a meth addict," Kevin muttered.

"Maybe, but Kenny is growing stronger by the day." Anna closed her eyes and breathed deeply the smell of Kevin's shirt. All was well in her world, and she could truly relax for the first time in months.

The fragile peace between brothers was shattered three days later when Kenny's Cobra careened off a bedpost and ended up under Robert's bed while Robert was at a doctor's appointment. Kenny, who was deathly afraid of spiders, asked his father to retrieve the car. Instead, Kevin pulled a black leather shaving kit from under the bed. It was zipped tight, and Kevin knew he should replace it immediately but couldn't. For a moment he stood holding the small satchel as though he were guessing the weight of a bag of apples. He hadn't seen or smelled evidence of cigarettes on his brother. There was no behavior indicating drug use in months. Robert had even refused to split a pitcher of beer with Kevin when they were at the pizza parlor. But fifteen years of disappointment caused Kevin to unzip the case. Inside were zip locked bags bulging with hundreds of different colored pills.

"Kenny, go downstairs," Kevin said, beginning to shake as he held the case well above his son's eye level.

"What about my car?" Kenny asked.

"Do as I say!" Kevin barked.

Kenny backed out of the room, fighting tears as the door slammed in his face. Kevin's face, a mask of fury, went to the closet, grabbed Robert's duffel bag, and began to cram it full of Robert's clothing and personal items until every belonging and evidence of Robert's stay was erased from the room. In disgust, Kevin even stripped the bed and threw the linen down the laundry chute.

When Robert pulled to the curb twenty minutes later and saw Kevin sitting on the porch next to his duffel bag he felt certain Kevin knew. As Robert walked slowly up the driveway, trying to find the words to explain, Kevin grabbed the duffel with one hand and threw it at him. Surprised and so much weaker was Robert than his brother, the blow knocked him down, and the heavy bag settled on his chest.

"It's not enough to be a junkie! You've got to be a dealer too!" Kevin exploded.

Robert struggled to roll the bag off of him. He sat up looking at his seething brother through hurt and confused eyes. Kevin continued, "You bring this crap into my house?" Kevin held up the black satchel. "You bring this around my sick child? After all I've tried to do for you?"

"It's not what you think," Robert stammered.

"No, of course not. This is probably just candy."

"It's not candy. It's.." Robert didn't get the chance to continue as Kevin threw the bag at him and followed up by lifting him to his feet by the lapels of his jacket. The black bag fell to the cement, a few pills rolling to the lawn.

"I don't give a damn what it is," Kevin said holding Robert close. "We're finished. I don't ever want to see you again. I won't have you around my son." For a moment the brothers starred eye to eye, both men pale, a thin sheen of sweat breaking on each brow. A thin trickle of blood trailed from Kevin's nose, and for an instant Robert wanted to wipe the bad blood between them away. Kevin released Robert. "Now get the hell out of here."

Kevin turned back toward the house suddenly exhausted, his feet heavy and head light. He saw Kenny looking through the window and wondered briefly if he had seen everything, before averting his eyes to his own feet. Robert stooped weakly and retrieved the satchel and duffel. With effort he shouldered the bigger bag before heading to the trunk of his car. Kenny watched his uncle drive away, tears streaming from both faces.

The nosebleed that took better than an hour to stem was similar to the one that had spelled the beginning of the end for Kenny's grandfather. Kevin pushed this from his mind, sure that the stress Robert had caused him was behind the trickle. Subsequent nosebleeds, however, could not be dismissed, and Kevin soon found himself awaiting blood tests that would confirm what he already knew.

When the diagnosis came Kevin found it curious that he was not as devastated as he would have imagined. It had been far worse when the same physician had pronounced Kenny's condition. Perhaps he had always known it was coming and had resigned himself to an outcome that could not be avoided. If there was any consolation in the ordeal it was seeing Kenny continue to thrive and flourish after the doctors declared a clean bill of health for the boy.

The roles now reversed, Kenny came to see his father in a room much like the one he had escaped two months earlier. Anna, ever the pillar of strength, unfailingly brought Kenny after school, and the family had dinner together each night, mother and son eating fast food from bags and Kevin nibbling at bits of hospital food in an effort to put on a strong front. Both parents helped Kenny with homework in an effort to make up for lost time incurred during his own bout with the disease that had apparently forsaken him in favor of his father.

One night, Kenny left the red Cobra on the tray table at his father's bedside. Kevin held the car up to the light and thought of Robert, wondering where he was and what he was doing. It would, no doubt, have surprised Kevin to know that Robert, at that very moment was standing in the rain outside the hospital, looking up ten stories to Kevin's window. The rain coming down, cleansing his face, reminded Robert of his youth before his father died, of looking skyward when it snowed; how easy it was to imagine flight. Robert's hands were clasped in prayer as he murmured, begging that it be he who carried the burden of the disease rather than his brother. Rain and tears mixed, trailing through thin patches of facial hair.

In a fashion eerily similar to the way that the disease had abandoned Kenny, Kevin's counts began to improve within days. Doctors huddled, wondering if some genetic miracle were in play. Lightening striking twice didn't seem possible, but the results of Kevin's tests were irrefutable. Ten days later, Anna and Kenny were helping Kevin into the car with the assistance of a kindhearted nurse.

Father and son were strapped in, and Anna was about to get in the car when she paused for a moment. She looked at her purse, shut the door, and walked back toward the hospital in pursuit of the nurse. "I'm sorry to bother you," Anna began, as she approached the startled nurse, "but I had a question you might be able to answer."

The nurse looked puzzled as Anna dug through her purse before producing a clear sandwich bag that held a single pill. "I was wondering if you could tell me what this is?"

The nurse opened the bag and took out the pill before holding it closer to her eye. "It's called Efavirenz. Some call it Sustiva. Where'd you get it?"

"I found it on my lawn," Anna replied truthfully. "What's it for?"

"It's a component of an HIV cocktail, the nurse answered pleasantly. "Would you like me to dispose of it for you?"

St. Vincent's Medical Center and the Centennial Assisted Living Center were across the street from one another but shared much of the same parking. And while the morgue in the basement of St. Vincent's saw its share of patients from both facilities, each boasted of patients leaving under happier circumstances as well. The elderly being released from St. Vincent's quite often went into permanent residence at Centennial. The few geriatrics that emerged from Centennial with pulses usually did so in a matter of weeks after gaining strength following a stroke. These fortunate few were sent to the Stroke Rehabilitation Center (SRC) with hopes of regaining enough use of their limbs to allow them to go home where they could enjoy what remained of their golden years. The SRC only admitted patients they thought could endure and benefit from the rigorous therapy that would yield the sought after results. Most stroke victims, quite simply and sadly, did not have the potential to enjoy the success rate the SRC produced. As the two facilities were under the same management, they worked quite well together in coordinating seamless transitions.

Angela had just sat down after putting cream and sugar in her coffee, when she saw Mrs. Davine enter the cafeteria. The woman was all business and made a beeline to the corner table at which Angela sat waiting. Opening her shoulder bag before she even sat down, the older woman placed a notepad on the table as she offered Angela a perfunctory smile and nod of her head.

"Good to see that you're right on time, Angela,"

Mrs. Davine said, glancing at her watch as if it could just as easily indicate that Angela was late. Angela was, in fact, early and had made a point in being so. Mrs. Davine unsheathed a pen and feasted her eyes on the tablet in front of her.

"Would you like to get something to eat before we begin?" Angela asked, suddenly aware that she had victuals and Mrs. Davine did not. "The pasta here is to die for." Mrs. Davine looked up frowning. "It's angel hair," Angela added meekly.

Mrs. Davine softened a bit. "No thank you, dear. I'm quite alright."

"Did you hear about the plane going down this morning?" Angela asked, troubled by the thought of casualties.

Mrs. Davine nodded, her eyes watering slightly. "The Lord works in mysterious ways. It's not for us to question his plans," was all she could bring herself to say. She cleared her throat and glanced at Angela's virgin tablet.

Angela got the hint, clicked her pen, and began dating the top. "July eleventh, two thousand and ten."

"The year of our Lord," Mrs. Davine continued, when Angela did not.

"Yes, of course," Angela smiled. It occurred to her that Mrs. Davine had quite possibly spent more time in church than she, Angela, had lived."

"Now then, Mr. Bingham," Mrs. Davine began.

"Yes. Mr. Bingham," Angela repeated, furrowing her brow in earnest. She wanted to be taken seriously and already regretted wearing a springy white and yellow dress, so very much unlike the somber navy blue suit her counterpart wore. Angela continued, "Mr. Bingham has been at Centennial for a little over three weeks. During which time he has demonstrated remarkable progress. Far better than we expected when he first got there," Angela noted.

"Yes. It's at this stage when people realize the deleterious effects a lifetime's habits have on a body," Mrs. Davine said, with just a trace of disapproval in her voice. Angela smiled as she recognized *deleterious* from her word-of-the-day calendar - last Thursday, if memory served.

"To err is human," Angela gently reminded.

"I should say so," Mrs. Davine said in agreement. "It's like the cumulative effects of cholesterol. Every little transgression adds up to block the way into his heart."

"So you think that Mr. Bingham is really ready for the next step?" Angela asked hopefully.

"Well that's what we're here to discuss, certainly," The older woman replied.

A group of youths had dropped backpacks on the floor under the table next to the two ladies. One of the lads took off a windbreaker and placed it over the back of his chair before sitting down. He had a number of earrings and hair that featured streaks of purple. A black sleeveless shirt exposed skinny arms featuring a variety of tattoos. Angela couldn't help noticing one particular bit of ink that featured a crucifix. She smiled slightly. Mrs. Davine rolled her eyes when she saw the tattoo, after glancing at the boy in an effort to see what had distracted Angela.

"Are his spirits good?" Mrs. Davine asked, refocusing her attention.

"Well, it's never easy when your mind is sound, and your body betrays you," Angela replied artfully. "But he's been a very positive influence on some of the other patients whose prospects aren't nearly as good," Angela added sadly.

"The way it's always been," Mrs. Davine returned matter-of-factly.

"Poor souls," Angela said sincerely.

"Yes, for most it's pure hell," Mrs. Davine said dourly.

"I suppose this would be purgatory," Angela sighed, looking at her surroundings.

Mrs. Davine ignored Angela's comment, instead, asking point blank, "Do you think he can handle it?"

"I think of Mr. Bingham as being fairly adaptable," Angela replied truthfully.

"He'll have to be. It's a big change."

"His heart is strong enough?" Mrs. Davine queried.

"I believe it is."

"Good. That's half the battle," the older woman stated firmly.

"I think he deserves a chance," Angela said hopefully.

"Well, I suppose he's as good a candidate as any other you've recommended," Mrs. Davine said putting the cap on her pen.

Angela was not certain this was intended as a compliment.

The youths were joined at their table by a lean wiry girl with several piercings in her lower lip. She put an enormous piece of chocolate cake in the middle of the table and handed plastic forks to the two young men who began to dig in with zeal. Mrs. Davine watched for a moment wondering what had become of etiquette in recent years.

Angela noticed Mrs. Davine's attention had waned. "Have you ever had any?" She asked.

"What?" Mrs. Davine's attention turned back to

Angela.

"Devil's Food cake," Angela said smiling impishly.

"Not since I got this job, I haven't." Mrs. Davine smiled for the first time. "It does look tempting, though. I must say."

It appeared the gluttonous eaters were competing with one another as the end of the cake neared. "Goddamn dude! Slow down!" One eater accused the others. The smile on Mrs. Davine's face vanished instantly.

Angela winced slightly but pretended not to have heard and returned her attention to the notes she had taken. Mrs. Davine nodded her head in the direction of an elderly couple three tables away. They were taking turns eating bird-like bites from a light fluffy wedge of angel food cake, wiping their mouths delicately with each bite. "That's a little more to my liking," she said. "Doesn't weigh on one so."

"So it's settled? Mr. Bingham gets a chance to prove himself?" Angela asked, hoping to seal the deal.

Mrs. Davine nodded slowly as she scrutinized her counterpart. The girl was lovely, and while she had a great deal to learn, her heart was certainly in the right spot. She had been well placed as a liaison, and they were blessed to have her. The older woman reminded herself that the gain had been someone's loss. "Dear, I know it's poor form, and I hope you'll forgive my asking, but you're so young, and I can't help wondering, what caused *your* death?"

Long Lost List

This is real life I'm talking about here, not the movies. Just remember that.

In the movies, we eagerly accept a bend or warp on realities and the reactions our onscreen heroes have to situations, even as they differ markedly from what we think we might have done in a given situation. This warp, and the constant slew of hurdles that seek to derail our heroes, are after all, why we seek the solace of the theater in the first place. I get that. I also get that characters in the movies, both good and bad are equipped with just the right quip for all situations. This further differentiates them from the rest of us, who think of the perfect response while fuming in our cars half an hour after the opportunity has both come and gone.

If this had been the movies, things would have turned out much differently, I'm sure. As it is, they just turned out, almost as if they'd been predetermined. In the midst of a seemingly ordinary and uneventful life, in which the acquisition of a sports car, in lieu of an affair, seemed inevitable, I found myself reading the paper before heading out the door. I do this so as not to appear out of touch when my colleagues gather to talk sports, politics, or current events. I try not to express disbelief that they posses a far greater understanding of the former than the latter. At any rate, while washing down the cold English muffin Julie, my teenage daughter, had abandoned in favor of a fresh application of lip-gloss, I noticed a familiar name, if not mugshot, in the metro section. Coffee dripped from my chin as I tried to reconcile the name with the thumbnail photo of limited resolution just beneath the fold.

I had gone to school with a Eugene Redinger. Scanning the article for an age revealed this Eugene Redinger to be 42, just as I was. Which meant despite the photo, which did no justice to how I imagined my once best friend might presently appear, it could still have been Mean Gene. Mean Gene was a nickname much like the nomenclature Tiny, given to a three hundred-pounder. Gene was as passive as it got. So it was not for some gruesome murder that Eugene Redinger was identified in my morning paper. It appeared Gene didn't get out much, as the article indicated he had been a patient at the Rockview Sanitarium outside of Seattle for the past eight years. Eugene had always been socially awkward, but it appeared now that he was nearly catatonic.

So just how does a nearly catatonic, middle-aged patient removed from everyday society become front-page news? According to fellow patient Justin Gage, who was evidently anything but catatonic, Eugene had supplied the winning Lotto numbers in advance of the drawing for the second consecutive week. Justin was a bit vague as to how Eugene communicated these figures. Perhaps Justin felt he might need to go to that particular well again some day and wanted to make sure it was not mined without his involvement. At any rate, it seems that Justin had also experienced remarkable success this past football season when it came to beating spreads and picking winners.

My mind began to swim as I recalled a youth spent with Eugene Redinger. In junior high, we had been thick as thieves, two peas in a pod, practically inseparable. This came about largely as a result of our being neighbors, only children, and identified as talented and gifted in the areas of math and science. That we had no other friends probably contributed to the mix as well. Guys like us had to stick together out of necessity. I'll have to ask my daughter when I next see her if the terms nerd and geek are still used. Regardless, they were.

Eugene never saw himself as a nerd or a geek though. Kind of an, ignorance is bliss sort of thing, I guess. As a matter of fact, he thought of himself as a sort of Casanova, always trying to read girl's palms. I figured it was as close as he would ever get to actually holding a girl's hand, but I saw him do it plenty of times. This usually resorted in the rolling of heavily mascarraed eyes or peals of giggles, as Gene outlined their futures.

I put the paper down and wiped my chin. Eugene Redinger *had* claimed to know the future. It was his shtick. Most of the time kids thought he was trying to be funny, but he was adamant about it, and every once in a while it got him in trouble. Usually when a kid didn't like what Eugene saw in their future. Once, a kid asked him to predict if it was going to be a left or right that hit him next. Eugene said he couldn't tell, and the kid hit him with both.

All Eugene's predictions were for things far in the future, which the other kids saw as rather convenient. It frustrated him to no end, and he would tell me with a straight face that he couldn't see anything until. *Until..* I strained my brain to recollect what year he had used as the opening of his clairvoyant window. All I could remember was that the window was for an even ten years and that it began sometime in the next century. I had asked him what would cause his window to open and close. It was the closest I ever came to actually believing him when he looked genuinely confused and claimed to have no idea.

The summer between junior high and high school was my growth spurt, and after coaches and girls began to notice me I broke ranks. I still tried to keep my friendship with Eugene alive, but it was no longer the same. He never said it, but I'm sure he felt betrayed, as if the only reason I still reached out to him was that of pity. Looking back, I wish I could say there wasn't a measure of truth to this tacit accusation.

Despite our being neighbors, I saw less and less of Eugene in high school. I was always at practice, games, or out with my teammates and the girls with whom we consorted. My interests branched to literature while he was still obsessed with flying, time travel, and a girl named Katlin. His family moved three hours north to Seattle after graduation. The last time I saw him was when I came home to find him talking to my mom at our kitchen table. He was writing in my yearbook while he waited for me to come home. It was awkward when we said goodbye, and while he gave me his new address I don't think I ever used it.

I couldn't even be sure I read what he had written in my yearbook. I tried to remember and couldn't recall reading it or what it had said. This caused me to rise uneasily and seek the book that I hoped was still in a box with my letterman's jacket and plenty of mothballs. I sat on a chest in the attic thumbing through the yellowing pages of my nearly quarter-century old George Washington High School senior yearbook.

A forty-watt bulb illuminated a list in the midst of Eugene's farewell note, his unique scrawl taking up most of the second to last page.

1. change of heart
2. dream car no more
3. GWll
4. Lord Oscar
5. curse lifted
6. no kat
7. ♀ potus
8. dowvl
9. flying pig
10. wb
11. willson kills jan

I quickly scanned the list, which made little sense until I came to number five: curse lifted. Eugene had been a lifelong Boston Red Sox fan and along with legions of others, believed the decades long dry spell without a title was due to a curse placed on the franchise by the Bambino after being traded away in 1918. The Red Sox World Series win in 2004 had headlines across the country proclaiming the curse had been broken. I smiled as I read through the remainder of the list. The Sox had been bound to win with a payroll bigger than some country's GDP.

The rest of the list seemed unintelligible. I was about to close the book when my eye was drawn to the only word that was not written in blue ink. The word *potus* in the seventh item was written in black. I knew that potus was an acronym for President of the United States. I also knew the country had just elected the first African American to the office. He had gotten there by upsetting the heavy favorite, and wife of a former president. I had failed to recognize the universal symbol for female because a single line had been drawn through it, as if Eugene had revised it after seeing history altered.

Chills ran down my spine, and I began to perspire as I revisited the list looking for any other reason to believe my one-time friend truly had the ability he had always claimed. The only other item I could glean anything from was the second. Eugene's dream car had been a Porsche. He was obsessed with them and had pictures taped on his binder, school locker, and bedroom walls. While not especially artistic, he was constantly doodling pictures of the German sports cars. I could still picture an emerald green Porsche 911 sliding around a corner taking up wall space that could have been devoted to a swimsuit model. The smile on my face was short-lived as I recalled nearly three thousand innocent men, women, and children dying some eight years earlier. If Eugene had seen this, it was no wonder the car model had lost its allure.

No longer able to hold the yearbook still enough to read due to shaking beyond my control, I went downstairs and opened my laptop. The Red Sox championship fell roughly in between the September 11th tragedy and the 2008 election. The list appeared to be in chronological order and focused on the first decade of the current century. Googling events of the decade occurring between September of 2001 and October of 2004 convinced me that 'gwll' was probably the invasion of Iraq, or Gulf War Two, to some.

With Hurricane Katrina hitting the Gulf of Mexico the year after the pouring of champagne in Beantown, I was willing to bet that 'no' meant New Orleans. As if I needed additional convincing at this point I was only further numbed rather than surprised to find that the movie based on Eugene's favorite trilogy had won an Oscar for Best Picture in 2003. We had both read Lord of the Rings more than once. Focusing on the short span between the turn of the century and the terror attacks, I was able to cross the first item off my list after reading of the first artificial heart transplantation in Louisville, Kentucky.

My drive to work was one in which you arrive only to wonder how. You can't recollect even a second of the transit and are amazed you made it without incident. At least you hope you did. The list had consumed me. It was all I could think about. At least I wasn't obsessing about Julie going off to college with my best friend's kid anymore.

That same best friend and business partner, Bill Clark, popped his head in my office to remind me of a meeting after lunch. For a moment I considered sharing the morning's revelations with him. But I merely nodded. This thing was so crazy, that I had to be sure. Not that I wasn't totally convinced. It's just that I couldn't introduce this to anyone not involved without having cracked the entire list first.

Bill and I were close, as were our families. We'd been in business together for nearly a decade, and our kids were dating - not something I was crazy about, unable to imagine it ending well. He was a sharp guy and a fresh set of eyeballs, but I couldn't help feeling the list was personal. After all, it had been my yearbook. I took out a yellow legal pad and wrote out the list in order; *dowvl, wb, flying pig* and *willsson kills jan*, none of which made any sense.

I spent the morning Googling everything Warner Brothers in hopes of decoding 'wb'. Lord Oscar had been movie related. Eugene had loved movies. Well, sci-fi/fantasy movies, anyway. Nothing seemed to work. I got frustrated. This was so like Eugene, always having to be so clever. Nothing could be simple or easy. He always had to do everything the hard way. Reinvent the wheel. No wonder he ended up in a sanitarium. Guys like him just weren't wired for the real world.

The mind-numbing after-lunch meeting was uneventful until I returned to the conference table with a cup of what I hoped would keep me awake. I was on the other side of the table and glanced at my legal pad as I was rounding the table. Seeing the legal tablet with items eight through eleven upside down caused me to exclaim, "I'll be damned!"

Bill looked up, annoyed at my first contribution to a meeting he'd been carrying. "You have something you want to add, Jim?"

I picked up my tablet and clutched it to my chest. "General Motors is bankrupt," I declared.

"Your point being?" Bill looked at me more amused than annoyed.

"GM is insolvent, broke, *upside down*!" I said with what I'm sure was a grin seen on many a village idiot.

Bill muttered something about our firm's being lucky we weren't upside down with a partner like his. I merely sat and smugly crossed off number ten.

Items eight and nine were revealed in the span of a thirty second break in public radio programming that had been serving as background noise until I heard that the Dow Jones Industrial Average had regained half of the losses it had sustained since bottoming the previous fall at six thousand. This was followed by an update on Swine Flu reportings in upstate New York. I pulled over to the side of the road and pulled the legal pad from my briefcase on the passenger seat. *dowvl* was Dow six thousand, *vl* meaning six in Roman numerals. The flying pig business had to be a reference to Swine Flu.

My head reeled as I acknowledged the chronological consistency. Eugene had been everything he had claimed and maybe more. Big Foot, UFOs, ghosts, curses, ESP, Loch Ness; none could be confirmed. But this thing - this thing with Eugene was real beyond a shadow of a doubt! It was all there in black and white. My friend was truly clairvoyant. This was too incredible to keep to myself, but I didn't know what to do with it. It was the story of the century. I could take it to the press; maybe even write a book. And then it hit me. I still hadn't cracked the final enigmatic prediction.

willsson kills jan. willsson kills jan. It was somehow different from the others. Assuming *willsson* and *jan* weren't acronyms, it was one person killing another on a planet of seven billion. For all its wonders, Google was of little help on this one. I tried everything and came up empty.

I grabbed a beer from the fridge, popped the top, and leaned against the island in the kitchen. Taped to the fridge was Julie's chemistry test sporting a 97%. It was a little reminder of the fifty dollars I had promised her for an A. Little Julie Newton would be heading off to college next fall. Little Julie Allison Newton. J.A.N. I froze, and my head swam. My daughter was in danger. *This* I knew to the core of my being.

"You sure you don't know a Willsson? Think Julie, think," I asked, trying not to sound too concerned.

"I'm sure dad. Why do you keep asking?" Julie countered, her amusement turning to alarm as I had asked the same question repeatedly.

"Never mind. Can you think of anyone who would want to hurt you?" I asked in desperation.

"Dad, you're freaking me out. What's going on?" Julie asked, looking at me, worry now etched in her young face.

I held her by both arms. "Just answer the question."

"No. The only one hurting me is you," she said with trepidation.

I let her go and slumped to the couch while she grabbed her purse and slammed the front door on her way out. Who is willsson? Who is willsson, I kept asking myself. I didn't know a willsson of first or last name. All I knew was that I had to protect my baby, my daughter. I could never live with myself if something happened to her, especially if I could have prevented it. I didn't know how I was going to do it, but I needed time.

By the time I had driven to Bill's house I had a splitting headache. He offered me a drink, which I refused. "Ron said you had a fight with Julie."

"Did she call him?" I asked.

"Yeah, he's with her now," Bill replied sitting down.

"Not a fight. I'm just worried about her is all." I sat and exhaled deeply.

"What's going on Jim? You haven't been yourself lately," Bill asked with deep concern.

"I appreciate your concern. I really do. I just can't talk about it right now. I need some time. As a matter of fact, that's why I came over. I wanted to tell you I'm going to take the next week off."

I had expected a battle. I really thought Bill would launch into a diatribe about how he'd been doing more than his share for the past few months. Instead, he patted me on the knee and said, "Take all the time you need, Jim. I know you're going through a rough patch."

I smiled, relieved. Bill's wife, Karen, entered the room and smiled at me uneasily. I said I needed to be going. Bill walked me to the door. I stood on the front porch for a minute after he had closed the door. I heard Karen's nagging voice through an open window, "Don't forget to take out the trash, Will."

Cold sweat broke out in an instant for the third time in less than a day. I drove like a bat out of hell determined to find my daughter before *Will's* son killed her.

My therapist insisted that writing this down would help me to begin to cope. I'm not sure it has. I'm only sure of three things. The food here is bad, the meds are good, and being with Eugene again is like old times.

GEORGE WASHINGTON HIGH SCHOOL
1984 YEARBOOK

Jim,

Unless u undergo a change of heart, I suppose this is the end of the road for us. I've already packed for the fall. No more dream car posters. No Kat Wilson. Lord knows, it kills me to say, but breaking up with her last January was like a dark curse lifted for both of us. She'll probably end up chasing the Grateful Dead around the country with Oscar, window view obscured by smoke (failing to realize the pot u smoke kills precious brain cells). I can't wait to get away. GW'll see my return when pigs fly or hell freezes over, whichever comes 1st. I'll write u in the fall when I get settled. I hope you'll w.b.

Eugene

The One You Remember

As you approach middle age and beyond I suspect most Christmases begin to blend together in your mind. Pleasant memories mingling in a general sense based roughly on the ages of loved ones surrounding tree and table. At least, that's how I find it to be. But I also suspect there's at least one Christmas that sticks out in every individual's mind as being apart from the rest; the one you remember, I call it.

The drive to Sunriver had been quiet and tense, the unease due to more than icy roads normally merited. My mother and father were working through what my mother would later call a *dicey patch* in their marriage. Looking back chronologically, it seemed to me like a rat passing through the body of an anaconda that served as a timeline. Of course, to my dad it was merely a little bump in the road, a hiccup, a rough spot in life's highway, any phrase accompanying a smile and reassuring tousle of my hair. At the time, I was afraid they were headed for divorce like so many of my friend's parents, and I spent the drive alternating between scheming to keep them together and imagining what my second bedroom would look like in a world where my brother and I were shuffled back and forth, loving my parents and yet hating them too.

I could see that my father had it all planned out, the perfect Christmas that would unite us as a family, making our familial bonds stronger than ever. In his mind it would be a Christmas that Jimmy Stewart, Donna Reed, and Bing Crosby could only dream of. There would be carolers, sleigh rides, hot cider, snowshoeing, lights, and a beautiful tree if he could manage it. But like all my father's plans, it would not quite play out as he intended. That became evident as we began our descent from the summit halfway between Portland and Bend. The snow became dirtier, the wells around the Ponderosa Pines wider and deeper, the icy patches fewer and farther between as we continued shedding elevation according to the small green signs posted on the side of the road at irregular intervals. We slowed to thirty-five miles per hour as we made our way through the Warm Springs Indian Reservation, and I cracked my window just a bit, shocking us all with the warmth of the air that rushed in.

"So much for a white Christmas, Molly," my mother said in disgust as I rolled up my window.

"Well, at least we didn't have to chain up," my dad said with characteristic cheer. This was met with uniform glares, and he busied himself in an effort to find a central Oregon station that would resume the Christmas music he had insisted we listen to since departing from home. Soon, Brenda Lee's was the only voice heard as my mom leaned her head against the window buffeted by her tasseled snow hat.

By the time we reached Bend, it was raining in a perfectly vertical sense, each drop drilling holes into what little snow remained in an effort to chisel each bank and drift down to size. Climbing slightly as we neared Sunriver, the snow on the ground became more plentiful, but the rain promised to make short work of what remained.

Burl Ives was cut short as Dad turned off the ignition after pulling in the driveway. We all lugged our bags and an assortment of wrapped presents into the modest house while dad crumpled newspaper before placing it beneath the grate in the fireplace. Mom placed a box of food on the island in the kitchen and looked at my father incredulously. "Why bother?" she asked in disgust.

Undeterred, my father smiled at me. "Makes it cozy."

I wondered if it was these kinds of things that made her love him when they first got married. I knew that nearly everything he did lately drove her crazy. He was so positive and cheery all the time; it was like he got dropped into our lives from a Disney set where everything always ends well, no one ever dies, and conflict exists only to give people reason to further endear themselves to one another. I wanted to strangle him myself every now and then.

When I came upstairs after unpacking, my father was on the phone. "I recognize there is no snow, but do you have like… wagon rides instead? Same concept just using wheels?" My brother and I looked at each other wide-eyed and then at my mother who had just poured herself a glass of white wine. My mother smirked for just a second, and soon my brother and I were holding our hands over our mouths to stifle our laughter. My mother shooed us down the stairs, following close behind so the three of us could laugh aloud. The moment offered the first flicker of hope I'd had in several weeks that things might be all right.

I went for a walk while my father and brother unpacked boxes of Christmas decorations. The rain had lightened as I made my way to the North Store, and I counted the homes with cars in the driveway. The Sunriver Resort community was filling rapidly and would be at capacity by tomorrow night, Christmas Eve. Some were just arriving as my family had, some were returning from a day on the slopes of Mount Bachelor or a foray into the Deschutes National Forest involving snowmobiling or cross-country skiing. Others lived here year-round and held their breath for the duration of the two weeks surrounding Christmas and New Years when school was out and their beloved community was inundated by renters and those who owned the homes but chose to live elsewhere.

The parking lot of the North Store was crammed, and I watched as families trudged in and out carrying groceries, snacks, cases of beer, and pop. Smiles and laughter were abundant. I walked by a half dozen small Christmas trees leaning against the side of the store, several ice machines, and display stands featuring real estate magazines and newspapers ranging from the New York Times to the Bend Bulletin. Next to the stands were stacks of bundled kindling for five dollars a bundle. I smiled as I remembered my dad boxing wood scraps at home this morning, intent on saving the five dollars he had been so chagrined at spending last year.

In between the trees and ice machines, the only homeless man I had ever seen at Sunriver sat with his back to the store's exterior wall, his legs splaying slightly beyond the trees and machines. He had on an old, well-worn wool coat buttoned up to his chin, long enough for him to sit on and probably quite nice when new. In addition, he wore a tweed cap I imagined more suited to an Englishman with a pipe in his mouth and a shotgun draped over an elbow. The man pleaded with eyes that were above a prominent nose and scruffy silver beard, the silver overwhelming the minority of coal black whiskers that had reluctantly given ground over time. Slender fingers stuck out of fingerless gloves the man used to hold what looked to be a dented dog dish containing several coins and a crumpled dollar bill.

The man looked curiously out of place, and I stared at him a moment, wondering how he had even gotten here. Bend was a dozen miles to the north and La Pine was at least that far to the south. Most people ignored the homeless man, walking by him as if he were yet another exterior display. A few people, usually coming out of the store, tossed a few coins or a bill in his dish while doing their best to avoid eye contact. I watched as the man snatched any new bills out of the dish and deposited them in his coat pocket with a practiced legerdemain. I wondered about the differences in the people who walked by the man as if he was invisible and those who gave him money. Did those who walked by simply not care? Did those who gave money do so out of guilt, knowing they were off to enjoy the luxurious status of those insulated by family and good fortune? Did they give out of kindness, pity, empathy, or perhaps a riddled combination? I had seen my father stop and fish around in his pockets for what seemed to me like hours, before giving a few coins to people on the streets of downtown Portland. I wondered why he did it, had never asked, and suddenly found myself curious.

I stood outside under the loose loops of Christmas lights and stared through the expansive windows featuring painted snowflakes and candy canes. It was like looking into an aquarium that you wanted to enter; swimming, cavorting, and mingling as if you belonged, all the while knowing you didn't. This was confirmed when I saw a girl I recognized from last Christmas. I had been watching my brother learn how to skate at the village rink. He was fearless and undaunted despite numerous falls that reminded me of Bambi on ice. I sat sipping a hot cocoa at a table near the edge of the rink missing my cousins and begrudgingly admiring my brother for the courage to try, knowing I was held back only by my unwillingness to allow anyone to see me make a fool of myself. A small cluster of girls at the table next to mine began snickering, and I realized they were laughing at Mathew.

I looked at them and was about to say something when one of them asked me where I was from. Whatever I was going to say in defense of Mathew dissolved in my throat as I answered, "Portland." At that moment, I wanted nothing more than to be in their group as it occurred to me that these girls had no idea I was a friendless bookworm back home. They invited me to sit with them, and for the next twenty-five minutes I sat and listened, privy to people I'd never been exposed to before, all the while hoping my brother would not come over or even wave to me.

The girls were from Lake Oswego and Forest Hills. Full of disenchantment with their parents, some were distraught at being forced to accompany their parents to Europe again next summer. One girl claimed it was her third time, bitterly questioning how, "anyone could enjoy going through museums day after day." I prayed my face didn't betray my thoughts as I almost died inside upon hearing this. For the past year, since doing a report on Venice, I had dreamed of going and had declared to my mother my intent to live there when I was grown. Another girl complained about her au pair, insisting the young woman had facial hair and the personality of a turnip. A third girl boasted of getting her housekeeper fired for stealing. The girl leaned close and whispered conspiratorially, "She wasn't really stealing. I just didn't like her." My stomach had churned at hearing this, but I was in too deep now and forced myself to weakly imitate the giggles I heard on both sides of me. It turned out all the girls would be in Sunriver for the next week, and one of them wrote her phone number on the back of my hand, insisting that I join them for sledding on Christmas Day. Thankfully, they left before Mathew grew weary of falling.

That night, I allowed the ink to run off my hand as my brother and I did the dishes. He looked surprised and then feigned disgust as I kissed him on top of the head in a pathetic attempt to purge my guilt. Cleansed of the ink, I still felt stained and weak for not defending Mathew. Even worse, I imagined some poor lady looking for another job with no reference from her most recent employee whose daughter "just didn't like her." All my favorite characters in my favorite books had one thing in common; character. I thought of Les Miserables, Francie Nolan, Sidney Carton, and the sacrifices they had made. My punishment for my lack of character would be to deny myself the fun of sledding with the girls, but even this felt hollow because I questioned how much fun it would really be, feeling as I did.

I had decided against going into the store and had turned away when a voice from the other side of the row of scraggly trees asked if I had changed my mind. I looked down at the man who was seated with the dog dish in his lap and a smile playing on his mouth. I shook my head no and began to walk by in the direction of the path that would take me back to the house.

"Can you spare some change, miss?" he asked with a rasp in his voice.

I froze, unsure of what to do. It hadn't occurred

to me that a beggar would ask money of a girl not yet thirteen. I reached inside my pants pocket and felt the five-dollar bill I had gotten for allowance the previous day. It was all I had, and I wished I had brought a quarter or some small amount of loose change. I compounded my mistake by looking at the man. Our eyes locked, and in the same instant I thought about running away I thought about how cold the cement must be under the tail of his wool coat. Slowly pulling the Lincolned paper from my pocket, I walked over and leaned to put the money in the dish he gladly extended, never taking my eyes from his. I don't know about the eyes being a window to one's soul, but I could see something lively and quick in this man's eyes. Something I was almost certain spoke of character.

When he mumbled, "God bless," I forced a smile and walked away.

It was beginning to darken as I walked home knowing that I would be expected back before dark. I was trying to decide whether my encounter with the old man reflected character or weakness when I saw from afar the Christmas lights on our house turn on, the deck a row of white icicles, the peak of the roof multi-colored. Lights on other houses could be seen, but it seemed as if ours burned brightest, and I stood still, looking at the house, seeing it in a way I hadn't ever before.

Most of the people who made Sunriver their home were retired and spent the months following Christmas snowbirding near Palm Springs, Arizona, or even Florida. Other homeowners used their houses as vacation rentals, spending an occasional week doing repairs during the off-season. A third group owned the homes as second or even third homes. I gathered that the girls I met while watching Mathew acquire bruises fell into this third category; what I referred to as the wantonly wealthy after discovering the adverb in an Austen novel.

Despite our having a vacation house, I knew we weren't among the wantonly wealthy. Far from it. As a matter of fact, money troubles were the source of my parent's marital strife. The house I was seeing in a new light was purchased by my dad and his brother after their mother died. The plan had been to have a place where both families could nurture childhood memories, getting together to celebrate holidays and birthdays, interspersed between work parties to maintain the place. They rented the house out enough to pay for property taxes and utilities. Neither my dad nor my uncle trusted the stock market, and they bought the house with the understanding that they would sell it when my brother, cousins, and I would go off to college. If the house appreciated even modestly while our families enjoyed it for better than a decade then all four of us kids might have our college paid for, graduating without debt, which was what my parents referred to as the greatest gift they could give us as we left their little nest.

I didn't understand terms and circumstances my parents bandied about as their discussions turned to heated arguments; phrases like *co-executor, 1031 exchange, capital gains, arbitration,* and *right of first refusal* meant little to me. But I did understand that a rift had developed between my dad and uncle involving taxes due in April. It had been two years since we had spent Christmas with my cousins in Sunriver, and it saddened me as I realized my cousins, Suzy and Amber, would have dragged me onto the ice where we would have giggled endlessly while falling all over each other, oblivious of stares or even the presence of any others. Both families still used the house, just never at the same time, calendars filled out in an exchange of terse emails.

I could remember how fun it had been house hunting, our two families crammed into my uncle's van as we made our way from one open-house to another, the cousins staking out would-be rooms in each house. After seeing a half-dozen we had all gone out to lunch. I had been so excited; I remember the pizza we ate had been tasteless, as if all my taste buds had dedicated their efforts in deciding on the perfect house. The place we all agreed was the most perfect was a split-level featuring a great room with a peak of windows overlooking the forest, a river rock fireplace and a huge deck with birdfeeders hanging from each post. It was far and away the nicest house we looked at in our price range, with only one catch. Less than a hundred feet behind the home stretched railroad tracks moving from north to south along the eastern edge of Sunriver. We decided to park the van in the cul-de-sac and wait for a train to come by so that we could judge how great a pitfall the tracks provided. After an hour we could hear the train approaching from the north, having rifled through Bend just minutes before. We spilled out of the van and remained silent, each of us equipped with our own tolerance gauge. The sound was larger than life as empty Burlington Northern and Union Pacific cars rattled on by, the graffiti they displayed as out of place as a homeless man against the backdrop of this affluent enclave. It was louder than any of us had imagined, yet we talked ourselves into buying the house all the same, reasoning that we would grow accustomed to the sound in the way that the people of Albany no longer noticed the pungent stench of their paper mills.

As I stood reminiscing about that day, it occurred to me that the homeless man may have hopped off a passing train, and I wondered momentarily if I would have the courage to leap from a moving train. It was hard enough to imagine asking people for money for food.

After my mother and father gently scolded me for cutting it close regarding daylight, we ate dinner, did the dishes, and sat in the great room enjoying the fire. A television was hidden behind sliding cabinet doors, but I don't think I ever saw it turned on. My father and Mathew worked on a thousand-piece puzzle that had been left half finished from our last visit. I knew Suzy and Amber contributed a few pieces during their stays in an effort to maintain a connection because we wrote little messages back and forth on the underside of some of the pieces; silly stuff like, *Amber eats kitty litter*, or *Molly loves Bad Brad*. My mother and I sat like bookends, curled on opposite ends of the couch reading novels. I looked at her and wondered if she knew how proud I was when people told me I resembled my mother.

That night, I dreamed I was homeless and on the streets of Portland holding out a coffee cup in hopes that passersby would contribute money. None did, and I could feel warm tears cascading down my cheeks as hunger gripped my ribs. It began to snow, and despite being empty the coffee cup would steam and hiss surreally as flakes landed in it.

Coming up the stairs the next morning, I smelled hope in the form of blueberry pancakes, my mother's favorite. I was greeted by my brother, who referred to me as 'Slug', our traditional tag for the last one to awaken, and my father who smiled at me with a twinkle in his eye. For the record, my father is the only person I knew whose eyes actually twinkle when he smiles. "You ready for a morning of snow shoeing?" he asked.

"I don't think we're going to need snowshoes to walk around out there," I said jabbing my thumb at the window over my shoulder.

He just smiled. "Probably not. I think we'll have to take a little drive."

My mother sat down in time to receive the first steaming stack of pancakes. "Your father and I think we should head up toward Mount Bachelor. There'll be plenty of snow up there." Their in sync decision-making fed my hope that my dad's master plan would work.

After doing the breakfast dishes, we loaded our snowshoes and sled in the back of the station wagon and headed for the mountain. As we ascended the patches of snow grew in size and soon interlocked for a modest layer that thickened as we neared the mountain. As much as we all loved to ski I was glad we had chosen to snowshoe today because it allowed for far more interaction. I had gotten a camera for my birthday the previous month and wanted to try it out with the snow as a backdrop. Straight out of my dad's plan, the morning was filled with laughter and talk, recollections of past Christmases, and even a shared story or two from my parents about Christmas memories formed before my brother and I had been born, each unafraid to interrupt with a detail or two when it occurred to them.

After an hour of trekking our way through the modest Ponderosa Pines we stopped for a snack, my dad sitting on a fallen log and taking off his backpack while my mother sat beside him. He withdrew twin thermoses and produced small collapsible cups splashed with primary colors. My brother and I sat on our sled while we ate our granola bars and drank the hot cocoa as our parents mixed coffee and cocoa for their own special blend. I ignored Mathew's look of annoyance after I stuffed my wrapper into his open coat pocket and took my camera from mine. My mom had inched closer to my father to allow him to pour without spilling, and after he put the thermoses away he put his arm around her. I hoped the picture I took of them sitting there was as good as I suspected, allowing me to surprise them by blowing it up and maybe even framing it. I also wished I could freeze or lock in place the happiness they shared at that moment, preserving it for all time.

As we resumed our trek we kept our eyes open for the perfect tree, which Mathew found in short order. It was nearly nine feet tall, straight, and evenly branched with a perfect top for our angel decoration. Without words, my father turned his back on my mother who unzipped his backpack and produced his folding saw, which resembled a giant pocketknife. He turned and she placed it in his hand as if he were a surgeon who'd called for a scalpel. I could see their eyes meet, and she reached up to kiss him. My brother and I turned away, embarrassed but pleased beyond words.

We all took turns as it became readily apparent that the saw sacrificed alacrity for its compact size. When the tree was finally severed from the stump that was left we placed it on the sled, careful not to disturb the natural direction of the branches. My parents reversed the process in returning the saw to my father's backpack, kiss included, and we headed back, our tracks providing direction.

Sunriver was brimming with capacity, and ours

was not the only vehicle sporting a freshly cut tree as we made our way through the many circles, past the array of festively lit shops that comprised the village mall, and north toward our house. We untied our tree and left it leaning against the house under the deck to dry out a bit and regain its shape while we walked around the mall after lunch.

I wondered if I would run into the girl I had seen the night before in the North Store. I was determined to be polite but demonstrate the character I had failed to exhibit when we had met. I would not laugh at, belittle my brother, or condone unkind behavior to anyone, even if I'd never met the person in question.

I soon forgot about the girl as my family made its way through the circular mall popping into most of the numbered shops, if only to say hello to the owners. My parents tried to support the small business people of Sunriver and sensed how tough it was to make a go of it by the mall's rapid turnover. We split up occasionally, my mother and I taking our time in the bookstores while my dad and brother looked at skis. When my parents were sampling red wines, Mathew and I checked out the skating rink, my brother becoming excited as I promised to skate with him on one of the days following Christmas. I could tell he loved the idea of teaching me something, the skate being on the other foot, so to speak.

I looked across the center of the circle, its red bricks in a herringboned pattern, people in bright scarves and mittens walking arm in arm laughing while steam wafted from their drinks. I took out my camera and waved to my mom and dad, each having emerged from a wine and cheese shop bearing a bottle. My dad pointed to the coffee shop as if to alert me to their next stop. I snapped a picture but got their backs as they turned into another small building. Mathew was retying the slick laces on his new boots for the fourth time, and I sat on a bench and scanned the village, taking in all the lights and cheery people. I wished my camera had a wider lens that would allow me to capture the entire panorama, a scene that included none of the ugliness of war, disease, racism, or poverty that filled the pages of every social studies book I'd seen. I closed my eyes and sought to freeze the image into my brain, but a picture of the homeless man from the night before floated into my mind. I opened my eyes and found upon doing so that the scene had become slightly tinged, like when a cloud passes before the sun.

Mathew and I got into the car, and my father turned on the heat, as it had grown noticeably colder since we returned from the mountain. Mom began to delegate chores in preparation for Christmas Eve. Dad was to build a fire while she prepared turkey sandwiches, and Mathew and I brought the tree up into the great room where we would help Dad put it in the stand. In accordance with my father's plan, after dinner we would all decorate the tree and drink hot cocoa while we marveled at its splendor; Christmas music faintly playing in the background, like some Rockwellian scene.

I knew that the day, perfect to that point, had gone off script when I saw my brother's face as he came in from checking on the tree. He looked torn between laughter and tears when he reported to my parents that our tree had been stolen. The smile vanished from my father's face as he realized my brother wasn't kidding. We all went out and looked. Pine needles. Not even tracks since there was no snow. Our perfect tree: gone. Vanished.

"Who would steal a Christmas tree?" my mother uttered in disbelief before adding, "On Christmas Eve."

It would take more than a Grinch to dampen my father's enthusiasm. "Mathew, you make the fire. Molly and I will procure another tree," he said, as if convinced there were a plethora of trees to be found as the sun was setting on Christmas Eve.

My mother shook her head and walked slowly up the stairs where she poured herself a glass of wine, her festive mood shattered. I put my jacket and gloves back on and got into the station wagon, waiting in the cold to see what extemporaneous miracle my father had up his sleeve.

We drove back to the village but didn't even get out as we saw the lights had been turned off, allowing employees to spend the evening with their families. Darkness set over both the land and my father's face, making him look old for the first time ever, the lines in his forehead furrowed while he hunched over the steering wheel as if he had trouble seeing. I felt badly for him, knowing how carefully he had planned, only to have Mr. Murphy and his malevolent law beckon once again. I reached for the radio dial and gave him a cheesy and exaggerated smile. We both broke into laughter within two notes, recognizing Bing Crosby's sleepy voice dreaming of a white Christmas. All the tension was broken, and my father reached over and tousled my hat.

"There were a couple of trees last night at the North Store," I offered meagerly. Steering in that direction I recalled the trees - all sparse, dry, and under six feet. My father and I joined Bing and bellowed out the lyrics with a desperate sincerity.

As we approached the North Store I could see two trees remaining, both about my height. I could also see the homeless man from the previous evening. The dented dish at his side, the man's arms were folded, and his coat was buttoned all the way up to his whiskered throat. The people who walked in and out of the store seemed in a hurry, likely picking up last minute items much like ourselves, and few paid him any heed. I avoided his eyes as my dad and I approached our two spindly choices. My dad's brow furrowed once more, and he focused on the trees as if the decision were one in which the right choice just might save his marriage. I offered little help, standing there with my hands in my pockets, seeing very little difference between the two scraggily trees.

"I wanted to thank you, miss," the man seated to the right of the trees said, the rasp still in his throat.

I smiled awkwardly, wondering if he was going to ask me for money again. My dad snapped out of his tree trance and looked at the man as if seeing him for the first time. Bewildered, my father didn't seem to know what to make of what the man had said.

The man directed his gaze at my father. "She gave me," he stopped and tried again. "Your little girl gave me five dollars yesterday. I wanted to say thank you," he explained.

My father turned as if now seeing *me* for the first time. "You gave this man your entire allowance?"

I nodded, uncertain if he was disappointed or proud. More than once I had heard him exclaim, "A fool and his money are soon parted," for the benefit of my brother and me. My father broke into a still-perplexed smile, pulled out his wallet and produced a five-dollar bill. "I'll match her contribution," he said placing the bill into the dish.

The importance of the choice between trees seemed suddenly diminished, and my father hastily grabbed one and brought it inside to purchase. Because of the tree's diminutive size we didn't need to lash it on top and simply put it in the back of the station wagon before getting in ourselves. My father turned the ignition and my favorite Christmas tune, *The Little Drummer Boy*, started playing low and solemn. Leaning his forehead against the steering wheel he clenched, my father scrunched his eyes and drummed his fingers; I was certain he was trying to think of any other last minute item we might need to preserve his plan.

"Wait here," he finally said, turning up the heat for me. The angle he cut toward the store had him missing its sliding door, and my stomach felt like a caldron of acid had tipped within it as my father approached the homeless man once more. I hoped he was going to give the man more money, repressing a sliver of fear that had my father rebuking the man for taking the whole of my allowance. Instead, after doing neither, my father reached for the man's hand and pulled him to a standing position. It wasn't until both men began walking toward our station wagon that the rest of the boiling caldron spilled within me.

My mind reduced their strides to slow motion, and I could see the irreparable undoing of my father's plan and ultimately our family knot. Neither the absence of snow nor the tree being stolen had been his fault. For all I knew, my parent's financial woes might not have been his fault. But this was sabotage, pure self-inflicted marital suicide. The last thing my family needed on an evening when cohesion and healing were in order was a foreign agent introduced to the delicate balance that was our familial Petri dish. Surely my father could see that.

The man started to open the door behind me, and

I could hear my father insist that he sit up front with us. I scooted toward my father who was shutting his door. "Molly, this is Walt Shermer," my father said as if introducing me to one of his old friends. "Walt, I believe you've met my daughter, Molly."

"Pleased to meet you formally, Molly," the man said after he'd shut his door. I forced a smile, and my chapped lips hung up on my dry teeth leaving the smile hanging unnaturally.

The Little Drummer Boy was finishing, and Mr. Shermer waited until the last note died before saying to me, "Always my favorite, Molly." I looked at him unsure if the gleam I saw in his eyes was real.

"Hey, it's starting to snow!" my dad said, turning on the wipers. As if on queue, the next song was, *Let it snow*. I looked at Mr. Shermer, and he winked at me, confirming that he was only the second person I'd known whose eye's twinkled.

"Making me all the more grateful to you, Paul," Mr. Shermer responded, looking out the window as the flakes tumbled slowly down around our car.

I hung back, fumbling with the twine on the tree as my father and Mr. Shermer walked up the front steps. I didn't want to see my mother's face when she realized my father had brought a complete stranger to spend Christmas Eve with us. I also realized this wouldn't be happening if I hadn't given that same stranger my allowance.

When I finally came inside, my mother wore a cold stoic mask that reminded me of the lady who cackled while pursuing more than a hundred Dalmatians for their fur coats. My mother had never been a yeller, instead becoming quiet and reserved, marshaling her thoughts for when they could best be expressed in piercing terms. After my father took his coat and hung it in the entry, Mr. Shermer helped my brother set the table. Mathew actually looked excited at the prospect of company and interesting company at that. My mother suggested she help my father bring in the tree.

"It's right here," I said, holding the tree at my side on the landing. "I brought it in." My words failed to fill the silent void produced by my mother's steely scrutiny of the scraggly sapling I was supporting with one still-gloved hand.

"Oh. Right," she said, glancing with darts toward my hapless father.

"Paul," she said coldly, "perhaps you can help me get the boxes of ornaments from downstairs."

"They're already up here," my brother chimed, as he came to look at the tree. "Hey, you stole Charlie Brown's tree!" he exclaimed, momentarily breaking the tension.

My mother used the brief lapse to her advantage, and a rapid clipped motion of her hand told my father to come downstairs with her immediately. "I think there's another box," she smiled icily.

I let them pass and brought the tree upstairs. Mr. Shermer helped Mathew and me put the tree into the stand. He and Mathew were on the floor turning the screws as I held the tree straight. The man was wearing a thin sweater over a white button-up shirt that had a faint grey ring around the collar. I leaned over and smelled Mr. Shermer, surprised that I could detect not even the slightest trace of alcohol, smoke, or body odor of any kind. I had never smelled a homeless person before but had imagined it would not be pleasant. He was quiet and uncomfortable as he smiled brittlely, not oblivious to the tension between my mother and father.

Soon my parents emerged from downstairs, and I could see a change had come over my mother, her demeanor readjusted yet again. She was putting her best foot forward and began to do her best to make Mr. Shermer comfortable. She offered him wine, which he politely refused, so she poured him a lime soda, same as she poured for Mathew and me, handing it to him with a smile that was both warm and genuine. I could only wonder what my father had said to her downstairs.

During dinner Mr. Shermer spoke little, treading lightly, interested more in observing I thought. I watched him as my father carried the conversation ranging from the snowflakes that appeared to be sticking on our deck, large and thick, to the economy and state of the businesses that occupied the village mall. The manners exhibited by our guest were meticulous and formal: he exchanged his salad fork for the longer tined version as he transitioned to the turkey that he cut into modest bites. I wondered what his story was, convinced he hadn't always been down and out. It saddened me to think a person could be alone in this world without a family, friends, or loved ones on Christmas Eve. It seemed particularly tragic to be poor, old, vulnerable, and with nothing to look forward to but declining health and the end of winter weather.

My mother had put on a red sweater before dinner, and I looked at her, wondering what if any fallout would follow Mr. Shermer's departure. She looked beautiful, her lipstick complimenting the sweater, and I noticed that she was studying my father, much as I had been examining our guest. Her expression was curious and familiar, and I realized it was the same expression my father had made upon learning that I had given Mr. Shermer my allowance.

As the meal came to an end, Mr. Shermer placed his knife and fork close together and left them hanging less than an inch over the edge of the plate, just as our grandmother had insisted Mathew and I conclude each meal. He began to thank us all for a lovely meal when my father put his hand on the man's shoulder. "Don't think you're getting out of here without tasting dessert. We lugged this apple pie all the way from Portland, and you won't taste a better pie than my wife's." Mr. Shermer seemed a bit ill at ease but nodded in acquiescence when he saw my mother beaming.

After dessert Mr. Shermer insisted on helping with the cleanup. Mathew and I cleared while mother made coffee and Mr. Shermer and Dad washed and dried the dishes nearly as fast as we could bus them. Soon, we were all sitting in the great room looking at the tree that Dad had placed on an end table in an effort to make it look more substantial. Mathew and I began digging through the boxes of decorations, which mostly consisted of ornaments we had made in school over the years. Mom had dated each one, a practice I once found silly but began to appreciate over time.

We drank hot cocoa and admired our modest efforts. The warmth of the fire had long since thawed me out, and I grew sleepy. I rested my head on my mother's shoulder and looked out the window where the snow was rapidly accumulating on the deck. I wondered how many homeless people at that moment were sitting on sidewalks or under bridges, their stomachs and hearts aching with emptiness. I wondered what would become of Mr. Shermer; if he ever had children, and if he had, were they thinking about him right now?

I must have fallen asleep because I felt my mother poking me gently in the ribs. "Time to go to bed, sleepyhead. You too Charlie Brown," my mother smiled at my brother, who looked as drowsy as I felt.

Even then, I breathed through my mouth when I slept, and it was dry when I woke. The alarm clock I used to awaken me when we skied read ten after eleven. I could still hear talking in hushed tones from upstairs and wondered if Mr. Shermer had gone. I went to the bathroom to get a drink, listening for his voice. I took my glass to the bottom of the stairs and could make out Mr. Shermer's voice along with my father's. My father was explaining how things had turned sour with his brother. I only caught the tail end of it but gathered my uncle had triggered something called a capital gains tax for which my father was ill-prepared. I marveled that this man whom I had known all my life, would open up to a complete stranger.

I heard Mr. Shermer express a measure of sympathy before telling my father he still had the most important things in life. He went on to speak very complimentarily of my mother, brother, and me. My father readily agreed, and it was quiet for a moment before my father spoke again. "I sense you've got some regrets in that department," he said referring to family. Mr. Shermer did not respond right away.

My father again broke the silence by offering Mr. Shermer some scotch. I could hear the bottle clink on the rim of my father's glass.

"No. Thank you, Paul," Mr. Shermer answered almost sorrowfully. "More than a few regrets, actually."

While I couldn't see my father's face, I felt certain of its countenance. It was a look that said, 'Go on, you can tell me, and I promise you'll feel better once you do.' It was a look that had extracted confessions from both my brother and me since we were small. And yes, I always felt better afterward.

Mr. Shermer continued after clearing his throat. “I had been clean for over a year. Hadn’t touched a drop or missed a single meeting. My marriage was revived, given a second go around I guess you could say. My wife and I stayed home a lot that year, didn’t socialize as we normally did. She was real good about that – keeping me out of situations that might tempt me.”

Mr. Shermer stopped, and I could picture my father nodding understandingly. “We’d gotten an invitation to a Christmas party we’d attended for years. The judge was a good friend of mine, and I hated to miss it. I told my wife I thought we should go. I can remember how dubious she looked, almost like that proverbial deer in the headlights. Probably didn’t want to discourage me, afraid it might show a lack of confidence in my conviction. Anyway, I convinced her it would be okay and that I had to go out into the real world sooner or later. Sure enough, she reluctantly agreed.”

There was a catch in his voice as he uttered the last sentence, and my father said, “You don’t have to continue, Walt.”

“Nonsense, Paul. You bared your soul to me. Why shouldn’t I do the same?” Mr. Shermer recovered. “The party was wonderful. Festive. I was enjoying catching up with people I’d spoken little to since I’d quit drinking. Of course, I hadn’t told anyone I’d quit, and I don’t think anyone even noticed. It’s amazing how adept you get at hiding it when you’re functional. And I was amazingly functional and prosperous for well over two decades, I have to say. Surprisingly enough, I wasn’t even missing it, just talking, laughing, listening, admiring the beautiful tree. Thing must've been eighteen feet tall. Splendid tree. Anyway, my wife approached me around ten and asked if I was ready to leave. Implored me with her eyes really. I think she wanted me to quit while I was ahead.

So I found the judge, shook his hand, thanked him for a wonderful evening, and told him we were leaving. He thanked me for coming and told me he had hoped to surprise me with a visit from an old friend we'd gone to law school with. Said the fellow had told him he would try to make it, but had failed to show.

My wife and I were just putting on our coats when the front door opened and who should appear but our old buddy, Thomas. Hadn't seen him since we'd taken the bar exam. I introduced him to my wife who regarded him warily. The judge was ecstatic, and the three of us got to talking. Thomas asked the judge if he had finished his book. This fellow had evidently left his practice to become a novelist. The judge insisted he had and enthusiastically recommended I read it. Thomas suggested he give me the copy the judge had just finished, and the three of us went upstairs to the judge's study to retrieve it. I told my wife, who had reluctantly taken off her coat and rejoined the party, that I would be back in a moment."

Mr. Shermer paused before continuing wistfully, "I can still remember looking down the stairs at her. I could see she was troubled, worried." He paused yet again. "The judge was looking through his library for the book while Thomas and I caught up. Before I knew it Thomas was at a small table holding a crystal decanter of scotch. I watched him pour three glasses. I knew I should say something. I wanted to say something, but I just couldn't make myself. The words simply would not come. It was almost like I was in a trance watching him pour the glasses in slow motion. The judge found the book and brought it over. He handed me the book and Thomas handed me a glass. The judge made a toast to Thomas's literary success, and we all clinked glasses."

"You don't have to finish, Walt. I think I know how your story ends," my father said quietly.

"You think I drove home drunk and crashed the car killing my wife," Mr. Shermer stated. My father mumbled something I couldn't make out. "No. That would have been bad, I'll readily admit. But that's not quite how it played out. My wife knew the moment I came down the stairs what had happened, and we left soon after. I didn't try to lie or pretend it hadn't happened. I just handed her the keys and got in the car, waiting to hear about it all the way home."

Mr. Shermer adjusted in his chair, and I shivered on the top stair before the landing, knowing I shouldn't be eavesdropping, that this was none of my business. His voice, much lower now, caught again as he continued, "But she never said a word. Just drove home hunched against the steering wheel, clutching it with both hands, tears streaming down her face. I never felt so small in all my life. We hit an icy patch, slammed into a tree, and I was left without so much as a scratch or even a goodbye."

Looking for something, anything to say, my father declared with a hollow voice, "She didn't suffer."

"No. Not then. But thirty years of marriage to an alcoholic…" Mr. Shermer's voice trailed into nothing.

"You can't blame yourself for the accident."

"I've tried telling myself that Paul. It doesn't

work. She hated to drive at night. Said her vision wasn't the same. She never would have gone if she'd known she'd be forced to drive," Mr. Shermer lamented. And then, almost as an afterthought, he added, "Especially during the winter." I imagined him looking out the window at the several inches of snow on our deck outside.

"It would be easy for me to tell you to forgive yourself, but we both know that's not for me to say," I heard my father murmur. After several minutes he offered, "You're welcome to go to church with us tomorrow."

"A first step toward forgiveness?" Mr. Shermer responded.

"Couldn't hurt," my father responded, and I didn't need to see his face to know the smile of kindness that adorned it.

Moments later, my father got a blanket and pillow from the bathroom closet and told Mr. Shermer he was welcome to spend the night on our couch. I went to back to my room and looked out the window. A layer of snow, glittering and pristine, blanketed the world outside, and while it was beautiful I saw it in a different light as I now realized the practical challenges it provided those without roofs over their heads. As I lay in my bed waiting for my body to warm the sheets and blankets I tucked in around me, I pictured Mr. Shermer with his friends, heavy-bottomed glasses poised in a toast. A moment of weakness he would remember and rue every day of his life.

I don't know why, but I was surprised to see Mr. Shermer sitting at the breakfast table drinking a cup of coffee when I came up the stairs the following morning. He had showered, combed his hair, and was wearing one of my dad's shirts. It became easier to imagine him as a successful attorney arguing in front of a jury, his voice soft but riveting.

"I've convinced Mr. Shermer to accompany us to church today, Molly," my dad said as he placed a plate of bacon on the table in front of our guest, Mathew, and mom.

"And then I'll have to say goodbye, Molly. Your family has been more than kind, and I can no longer impose." Mr. Shermer looked at me and smiled sincerely.

Our family attended Holy Trinity whenever we were in Sunriver on a Sunday. It was especially packed on Christmas Day. I sat in the pew, my brother on my left and only Mr. Shermer between the center aisle and me. Mr. Shermer stayed behind as we went to receive communion, his head bowed as we slowly made our way back to our pew. My father handed my brother and me each a few dollars to put in the basket, and I was tempted to hand a bill to Mr. Shermer because I was embarrassed for him, having to choose between giving up one of the dollars he'd secreted from his dish and refusing to contribute at all. To my surprise, when the basket came our way he reached for it, and for the briefest of moments I thought he was going to withdraw money *from* the basket. Instead, a small, folded envelope dropped from Mr. Shermer's palm into the basket. I suspected it was an envelope from inside the hymnal. I wondered if he had merely sealed an envelope in order to stave off the embarrassment of having no contribution of his own to make.

After we had filed out of the church my father offered to take Mr. Shermer some place, mentioning a soup kitchen in Bend as a possibility. Mr. Shermer politely declined, said his goodbyes repeating his heartfelt thanks, and began to walk in the direction of the mall that was still and quiet in the distance. As we headed toward the car to make the short drive back to the house I asked if I could walk home. Mathew looked at me strangely, but my parents merely told me to hurry, reminding me that we would be opening presents after lunch. When their car was no longer in sight I turned and walked in the direction of the mall, following Mr. Shermer at a distance, blending in with other walkers enjoying Christmas Day.

In the middle of January my family returned from one of Mathew's all-day Saturday basketball tournaments. My mother began to prepare dinner while my father got the mail. He came in fingering through the envelopes, his forehead scrunching as he picked out one in particular. After reading it the color drained from his face, and he handed the letter to my mother to read.

She too looked puzzled while reading aloud, "A twenty-five thousand dollar donation has been given to The Holy Trinity Church in the name of Paul Colson. The actual donor wishes to remain anonymous." She looked up at my father who was now grinning ear to ear. "What in the world?"

"Don't you see? We get the deduction!" my father beamed.

My brother and I looked confused as my dad attempted to explain how our tax bill would be greatly diminished as a result of the deduction. "Isn't that incredible?" he kept asking no one in particular.

That night my father called his brother for the first time in more than a year, talking and eventually laughing for over an hour. After he hung up I came into the kitchen and found my parents in an embrace. Once again, my father asked, "Isn't it incredible?"

My mother smiled at me. "Your father thinks Mr. Shermer's responsible," she said.

I smiled at them and walked out of the kitchen. *Incredible?* I thought. Maybe. *But surprising?* Probably less so if you'd followed Mr. Shermer to the store you first encountered him and seen the man reach into his coat pocket, pull out a wad of rumpled dollars, stick them all in the red Salvation Army pot before reaching into his other pocket, producing a set of keys that he used to unlock a sleek black German sedan while looking up and winking at you with eyes that *most certainly* twinkled ere he got in and drove out of site.

If you enjoyed these stories please check out other volumes of Twist's Tales at:
http://www.michael-twist.com/
Also, feel free to send me a comment at:
info@michael-twist.com

20463077R00096

Made in the USA
Charleston, SC
14 July 2013